The Hunting of the Nark

Sherlock Holmes Through the Looking-Glass

by

Claire Daines

Paperback ISBN 978-1-78705-618-3
ePub ISBN 978-1-78705-619-0
PDF ISBN 978-1-78705-620-6

Published by MX Publishing
335 Princess Park Manor, Royal Drive,
London, N11 3GX
www.mxpublishing.co.uk

Cover design and illustrations by Madeline Quiñones

To my brother Stu,

who ain't going anywhere until he's told every story he

wants to.

Contents

Author's Note

Since I first had the idea for this collection, I've often asked myself why Sherlock Holmes and Lewis Carroll seem to go together so well. Don't Holmes's methods rely on logic and natural laws? How does that fit in with the chaotic nonsense of Wonderland and the Looking-Glass world? If you look closer at those two worlds, however, it becomes clear that they do have their own systems of rules and logic, just not what a newcomer might expect. Not only that, but while rereading the White Knight's chapter in 'Through the Looking Glass,' I was struck by the Knight's uncanny resemblance to Holmes: his kindness and courage; his absent-mindedness; his complete ignorance about certain mundane matters; his interest in minutiae; his artistic streak; and especially the mood swings, Watson often having to help the detective back onto his 'horse' after a bout of depression. Doyle's version of Holmes can also be quite playful, and even downright absurd at times, however level-headed or logical he claims to be; and that whimsical streak easily allows me to imagine him actually *doing* some of the ridiculous things in Carroll's works. For that reason alone, the White Knight had to be allowed to take up residence in Baker Street for a time, much to the consternation of a certain long-suffering flatmate and landlady! I'll make it up to them later, I swear.

Claire Daines

The Hunting of the Nark

"Just the place for a Nark!" the Detective cried,
As he eagerly surveyed the scene;
With the stout-hearted Doctor alert at his side,
And the Dog standing guard in between.

"Just the place for a Nark!" Holmes repeated once more;
"I expect any second our man.
Fred Porlock has so rarely failed us before
In betraying our enemy's plan.

"His form is ungainly—his intellect small—"
(The Detective would often remark)
"But his courage is perfect! And that, after all,
Is a capital trait for a Nark.

"But oh, trusty colleague, I dread most the day
That our Nark be discovered, for then
He will softly and suddenly vanish away,
And never be met with again!"

They waited with patience, they waited with hope;
They waited 'til day had quite gone;
The sky overhead became heliotrope,
And the watchers increasingly wan.

Then the Doctor did yawn, "Must we wait until dawn?
I would rather not sit in the dark."
The Detective looked grave, and said, "Courage, *mon brave*,
We shall wait one hour more for our Nark."

But as darkness came on and the stars faintly shone,
The Detective, too, started to scowl;
"I fear you are right, we'll not see him tonight–"
When the Dog cut him off with a growl.

"Why, Toby, what is it? Our Nark come to visit,
With tale of nefarious scheme?"
The Dog merely frowned, then all jumped at the sound
Of a terrible, blood-curdling scream!

" 'Tis the voice of Fred Porlock! Quick, Watson, your gun!
We'll not leave our Nark to cruel fate!"

Detective and Doctor took off at a run,
Though they feared they would be far too late.

The Dog led them true to the spot, but they found
Not a wheel track, or footprint, or mark,
By which they could tell that they stood on the ground
Where once had lurked Porlock the Nark.

"Alas, all in vain!" groaned the Doctor. " 'Tis plain
Our Nark's met with some murderous lout."
"Then our mission is clear," declared Holmes, "for I fear
Moriarty has found Porlock out."

They sought him with Yarders, they sought him with clues,
They pursued him with resolute tread;
They brought him to justice with gambit and ruse,
Till at last the Professor fell dead.

You Are Mad, Sherlock Holmes

"You are mad, Sherlock Holmes," the Doctor said,
"I declare you have no common sense!
If a villain has put a large price on your head,
Why take only a stick for defence?"
"I shall paint my face white," the Detective did boast,
"Wear a sheet to the home of that crook;
Then if Gruner should see me, he'll think I'm a ghost,
And with ease I shall pilfer his book!"

"You are mad," said the Doctor, "I've said it before;
When a case will allow you no rest,
You steal all the cushions and sit on the floor –
Of what possible use is a nest?"
"Contemplating rebirth," Holmes replied with a stare,
"Is best done from inside a cocoon;
And now that we're after the missing St. Clair,
I confess that I've found it a Boone."

"You are mad," said the Doctor, "your antics of late
Would try the goodwill of a saint!
While a wax silhouette may be suitable bait,

Can't you see that your landlady ain't?"

"My own pistol," Holmes said, "has been cutting up stiff,

Since 'V.R.' earned her venomous glare.

Ricochet within miles of that critical sniff?

I assure you, no bullet would dare!"

"You are mad," said the Doctor, "your reason kaput,

Treating danger as naught but a joke!

Can you hope to discover this devil afoot,

With no mind left to go up in smoke?"

"Well, then I ask you, Doctor, how mad must *you* be

To involve yourself in my affairs?

Insanity's catching!" Holmes chortled in glee,

And galumphed down the seventeen stairs.

How Doth The Smooth Extortionist

How doth the smooth extortionist improve his study floor,
Back arched like a contortionist, the carpet red with gore.
How helplessly he seems to writhe, how faint his final breath,
And leaves behind a world more blithe, the better for his death!

The Jury and the Mouse

Holmes declared to a tar,
"If with me you should spar,
As you did with Sir Eustace, this whistle I'll blow.
Come now, smoke a cigar
And begin repertoire;
There is naught you can tell that I do not yet know."

Said the tar to his judge,
"Not one word will I grudge,
For I'd do all again and be proud to admit."
"Then let Watson be jury,"
Smiled Holmes, "for I'm sure he
Was never more suited your case to acquit."

Speak Roughly

Speak roughly to the trembling thief
That on your hearthrug wheezes;
No petty crook deserves relief
Who priceless treasure seizes.

I spoke severely to the thief
Who lost his prize to geeses;
He'll err no more, it's my belief,
And I'm not the police's.

Twinkle, Twinkle

Twinkle, twinkle, royal hat,
How I wonder where you're at.
Down below in cellar room,
Leading butler to his doom.

The Robbers' Quandary

"Will you walk a little faster?" said a Colonel to a spy;
"There's my brother's clerk behind us, through the fog I caught
his eye.
See how eagerly he follows, yet how little understands:
Ruin presses ever nearer, forcing me to steal the plans.
Steal them, deal them, steal them, deal them, steal away the plans.
Steal them, deal them, steal them, deal them, deal away the
plans."

Then the clerk came rushing up, and forced his way in through
the door!
Struggle ended with the young man still and lifeless on the floor.
"Poor, brave heart!" the Colonel groaned, "a good man dead from
sad mischance!
But remains the pressing question: can you duplicate the plans?
Can you, can't you, can you, can't you duplicate the plans?
Can you, can't you, can you, can't you imitate the plans?"

"No, I cannot copy all within the time," the spy replied.
"These three papers I must keep, the rest in this youth's coat we'll
hide.

Let the train bear West away, while I return in haste to France;

Try if you can stand to see him blamed for how you stole the plans.

Blame him, shame him, blame him, shame him, blame him for the plans.

Blame him, shame him, blame him, shame him, shame him for the plans."

Tweedledee and Tweedledum

Tweedledee stole Tweedledum
With horses shod like cattle,
For Tweedledee, the bastard son,
Knew father would not tattle.

But German master saw them go,
And caused a murd'rous blunder,
Which frightened wayward bantling so,
He fled to parts Down Under.

'Tis the Voice of the Yarder

'Tis the voice of the Yarder: I heard him declare,
"Of my masterful brain let all villains beware."
As a dog on a scent, so he follows his nose,
Arresting whomever he finds as he goes.

When a crime has him baffled, red herrings galore,
He will hasten his steps towards Baker Street door;
But when Holmes saves his colleague from public disgrace,
He takes all the credit for solving the case!

LESTRADE AND GREGSON

Baskermoor

'Twas gloaming, and the lambent moon
Waxed fulsome o'er the darkling moor;
Scarred fells with granite corpses strewn,
The wind their dirge to roar.

Beware the Baskermoor, my sons,
Whence loathly Hugo earnt his meed!
Dread tale I therefore charge thee con,
And ancient warning heed.

Yon lordling craved a peasant girl;
Vowed he to be the maiden's swain.
Fair prize he reft from cottier's hearth,
Then galloped home amain.

As bibesome horde disported late,
She durst descend the vine-clad wall.
Her gaoler, finding bird thus flown,
Began in rage to wrawl:

"Foul spirits of the world adoun,
My soul this night I gage to thee,
If I might but atake the wench
And make her one with me!"

He gave his hounds the maiden's kerch,
Rode out amid the savage hue.
Bemased, the squires thence called for mounts,
Their leader to pursue.

But soon cold ferdness on them came,
For o'er the moor their lord's black mare
Ran frothing at full tantivy,
Her saddle starkly bare.

Yet anoward the company rode,
And came alast upon a gill
Where Hugo's hounds stood, hackles raised,
Drade gazes fixed downhill.

And still three revellers durst draw near
Where hapless maid had fled, unwene;

But 'twas not hers nor Hugo's corpse
Mirked most that fearful scene:

A fenden hound, as swert as pitch,
Crouched over Hugo, een ablaze;
Wrest out his throat with bestious jaws
'Neath watchers' pallid gaze!

The Baskermoor then faced the squires,
Who left it, scrilling, to its feast.
Alas! No steed has yet outrun
A malison released.

For since that night, the demon hound
Has brought our line misfortune sore.
Pray God may shrive, my sons! Till then,
Stay off the bloody moor.

The Professor and the Private Eye

The fog was drifting o'er the Thames,
As yellow as pea soup;
While seagulls hovered hopeful, each
A feathered nincompoop,
Forgetting that to land was but
To vanish with a 'gloop.'

The day was dank as dank could be,
The lanes a sea of mud;
And poor folk cowered helplessly
In dread of monstrous flood,
For one in every dozen courts
Had cobbles stained with blood.

The Colonel and Professor walked
Through London's streets of grime.
They shook their heads and frowned to see
Such vast amounts of crime:
"If this were only organised,"
They said, "t'would be sublime!"

"The Chinese tongs, the Yakuza,

The Mafia and the Mob;

Our empire, too, needs men prepared

To murder, bribe and rob.

I wonder," the Professor mused,

"If *we* could do the job..."

"O criminals, come forth and hear!"

The Colonel did implore.

"Too long we've lived in hiding

From the long arm of the Law;

But here, at last, a chance for all

To even up the score."

The eldest eyed him warily,

Yet ne'er a word they said;

Such words seemed but a death knell

To the easy life they'd led.

Young upstarts must take care, lest they

Be found without a head...

But Moriarty's fame had spread

To north, south, east and west;

And from all over England came
The bitter dispossessed,
Agog to hear his words of cheer
And see their wrongs addressed.

"I thank you," the Professor said,
And shed a grateful tear.
"The time has come for all to speak
With pride of their career;
Your noble dark professions shall
Find weight and purpose here."

But while they celebrated
The fulfilment of their dream,
Soon Moriarty realised
His thriving new regime
Was up against a heinous threat,
Far worse than it might seem.

A meddlesome Detective
Had begun to snoop and pry,
And Moriarty's schemes had thus
Too often gone awry;

This Sherlock Holmes would rue his choice
To be a private eye.

Strong measures were required to crush
His enemy – but what?
With long deliberation,
The Professor hatched a plot
To make Holmes's name and rising fame
Diminished and forgot...

Holmes paced the carpet back and forth;
Where could the Doctor be?
He'd left just after breakfast,
And it now was half past three!
With Moriarty still at large,
Holmes feared some villainy.

Well-armed with stick and loaded gun,
Holmes left the flat in haste,
His mind awhirl with visions of
The dangers Watson faced.
Best friend and case at risk, but only
One could be replaced.

Before a warped and flaking door
A solitary sentry
Kept wary eye on passers-by,
Preventing casual entry,
With *Watson's hat* upon his head –
Absurdly element'ry!

But at that very moment,
Holmes was spotted by the guard
Who put his fingers to his lips,
His whistle shrill and hard,
And, in a trice, by grim-faced men
Escape was swiftly barred.

Holmes cursed himself, quite certain that
He'd be heard of no more;
But then the sentry stepped aside...
And opened up the door,
Revealing an unconscious figure
Lying on the floor.

Holmes hesitated not a whit,
Uncaring of the trap

(Although he started *slightly*
When the door closed with a clap!),
And in the dark, a well-bred voice:
"Good evening, my dear chap."

"Professor Moriarty,
What an unexpected treat!
It was so kind of you to come –
I hoped one day we'd meet."
"Too kind," replied his host, amused;
"The game is thus complete."

"Your race to Watson's rescue
Was so admirably quick –
It almost seemed a shame," he said,
"To play you such a trick!
Almost..." And Holmes heard clearly
A revolver hammer click.

"When Watson's found with gun in hand..."
"The Yard will think the worst?"
Holmes scoffed. "Lestrade would never..."
"True, but *what would happen first?*"

Holmes paled. A public scandal,
And *two* reputations burst...

A laughingstock Detective,
Lost forensic legacy;
The Doctor branded murderer,
Reduced to penury,
His practice and his writing
Smothered in their infancy.

"In that case, Moriarty...
I should say that you have won.
Congratulations, my dear sir,
It's been a pleasant run.
Now, Colonel, in your own good time?"
But answer came there none.

The Colonel aimed his pistol true,
Then saw in great surprise
That Moriarty raised a hand,
With gleaming, thoughtful eyes.
Although allowing Holmes to live
Would doubtless be unwise...

"And then they disappeared again?"
The Doctor shook his head.
"Till next time," the Detective shrugged,
Concealing his own dread;
'Twas clear why his respected foe
Did not *yet* wish him dead...

To the Real World

" 'Twas a case of claim-jumping, sir," Sherlock Holmes said
To Robert St. Simon, forlorn newly-wed.
"Let the lady explain her decision to flee,
Then dine with the Moultons, the Doctor, and me!"

But St. Simon departed, allowing the four
To partake of a supper sat three hours or more:
Pâté pie, five cold game birds, fine vintage from cellar...
And spend the next week with acute salmonella.

The Queen of Hearts

The Queen of Hearts was kept apart,
With peers forbade to mingle;
The Knave of Hearts, he played a part
To keep the maiden single.

The King of Hearts employed his art,
But let the Knave go free;
The Knave of Hearts, that vile upstart,
Would end on gallows-tree.

Hush-A-By Patient

Hush-a-by patient, in fear for your head!
Till the thieves find you, with care you must tread.
When the thieves find you, three times they will call –
Biddle and Hayward and Moffat and all!

Hurtful Loop

Beautiful Food, prepared with care,
Waiting for a thoughtless pair!
Who would such bounty not include
In plans for the evening? Beautiful Food!

Beautiful Food! Too soon grown cold,
Set before empty chairs untold;
Who in their senses would be so rude,
Choosing a *case* over beautiful Food?

Hoity Toity

Doyle's career was hitting a wall,
Pushed Holmes over the Reichenbach Fall;
Thought it was safe to pick up his pen,
Found himself writing his bane yet again...

A-lounging in a Chair

I'll tell thee everything I can,
There's little to declare:
Once in my mind I saw a man,
Legs crossed in easy chair.
A keen grey gaze at me he cast,
That seemed to pierce me through.
"Who are you, sir?" I said at last,
"And what is it you do?"

He said, "I get my exercise
By learning every street;
At times I go out in disguise,
My enemies to greet.
When peace abides on earth," he said,
"I cannot rest at ease;
But violent crime and secrets dread
Are guaranteed to please."

But I had studied all my life
To learn the healing art;
And having earned the surgeon's knife,

I would not now depart.

So, tempted as I was by such

Intriguing narrative,

I shook my head and said, "Too much!

'Tis no fit way to live!"

He smiled, "I hunt for truth with lies,

And tread where saints would fear;

No client too lowly to advise,

From king to mutineer.

I study ash and ancient scrolls,

And when I'm bored with that,

I fill the wall with bullet holes

To brighten up the flat."

But now new figures filled my brain:

Hussars, explorers, knights,

And pirates of the Spanish Main –

Of these, too, I would write!

"Have patience, sir," I said to him,

Convinced he'd soon forgive.

A snort escaped, his features grim:

"You ask me how I live?

I find existence flat and stale,
My mind upon me preys;
I need conundrums without fail
To occupy my days!
Oh, Scotland Yard may pay a call,
Or some disgruntled royal,
But little thanks I get withal –
What say *you*, Arthur Doyle?"

I heard his weary, scornful gibe,
And realised in shame
That every great man needs a tribe
Much more than fleeting fame.
To work again I put my mind,
And saw across the sea
An army doctor, worn but kind,
Brought home by injury.

How much of *me* was in that man
I should not care to say,
But thus, a partnership began
Which lives unto this day;
And while Holmes never speaks a word

Of thanks upon the topic,
He knows full well 'twas I who spurred
His Boswell from the tropics.

And now, if e'er by chance I hear
A haunting violin,
Or if my wilful children swear
They *shan't* take medicine!
Or if I take a limping step
Upon a flight of stairs,
I smile in something like remorse
For having started on this course,
My fame and reputation's source
A pair that Time could ne'er divorce,
As brave as two berserking Norse,
Humiliating London's force
With wit and cunning sharp as gorse,
A-lounging in their chairs.

The Silver Blaze Fiddle

"First, the debt must be fraught."

That is easy: his second wife's tastes will have brought it.

"Next, his loyalty naught."

That is easy: the prize for lost race will have bought it.

"Make sure sentry won't shout!"

That is easy, with drugged dish of mutton on table.

"Take the trusting horse out!"

That is easy, for only a dog guards the stable.

"Now bring forth the knife!"

That is easy, and will not take more than a second.

"Lame the poor beast for life!"

Ah, that is much harder than villain had reckoned!

For unlike the sheep,

The flare of a match earned a hoof to his head.

As ye sow, shall ye reap:

Far swifter than racehorse was trainer's life sped.

The Lion and the Unicorn

The Lion and the Unicorn were fighting for the crown;
The Unicorn jumped out the window, chased the Lion down.
Holmes saw a paragon, father saw a clown,
Cousin Mary saw her chance and skipped on out of town.

Paraphernalia

Some readers may be familiar with one of Lewis Carroll's longest poems, 'Phantasmagoria'. For those who aren't, a brief spoiler: a ghost visits a mortal, intending to haunt him, they become friends and discuss the bureaucracy of the spirit world... and then the ghost discovers he's actually got the wrong address. None of Holmes's cases seemed to suggest themselves for a parody, so I decided to change tack for this one, and let two underappreciated cast members have some behind-the-scenes face time!

One summer day, at half-past four,
　　Hot, tired, and cross, and sweaty,
I knocked upon my brother's door,
Resolved my troubles to outpour
　　While resting on the settee.

His landlady came into view,
　　White-haired, her kind eyes twinkling.
"Why, Mr. Mycroft! How d'you do?
Was Mr. Holmes expecting you?
　　I hadn't the least inkling!"

'Twas plain that Sherlock was not there,
    Nor was his faithful Boswell;
But Mrs. Hudson, debonair,
Insisted that I mount the stair,
    Assuring me all was well.

"It isn't likely I should turn
    You out in *this* heat, is it?"
She scolded me with fond concern,
And, much refreshed by coffee urn,
    I thus explained my visit:

"It seems an old colleague of mine
    Is shortly to be wed.
Since to attend I don't incline,
I feel I must myself assign
    To send a gift instead.

"However, since I've never set
    My sights on wedded bliss,
All my deductive powers have yet
To ascertain what gift to get
    In cases such as this!"

My hostess smiled in clear surprise.

"But why, then, should your brother –
A man whom wedlock mystifies –
Be better able to advise
    In this than *any* other?"

"Well... 'twas not *his* advice I sought..."
    Though I knew little of it,
The doctor's charm and manners ought
At least one woman to have caught,
    From which I hoped to profit!

"Therefore, you hoped he'd overhear,
    And kindly put two cents in?!"
I blinked, dismayed, at tone severe –
My reasoning the woman dear
    Had taken great offence in!

"Those two may share this humble flat,
    And many strange adventures,
But how do you presume that *that* –
And you a Whitehall diplomat! –
    The Doctor thus indentures?

"To take such liberties, young man,
        Is in the poorest taste!
Why, just imagine, if you can,
The perils in Afghanistan
        That poor soul must have faced...

"Long months of lingering at Death's door,
        Miraculously spared;
Then shipped back home from foreign shore,
Still haunted by that horrid war,
        But found no one who cared...

"Until your brother came along,
        For which I've Heaven thanked;
Their partnership in righting wrong
Has done so much to keep *both* strong,
        A bond most sacrosanct!"

I bowed my head, expression meek,
        Entreating her to pardon me.
For having come with scheme oblique –
Within the Doctor's mind to peek –
        She'd good cause to be hard on me!

'Twas true that Watson, trusting soul,
 Deserved of me far better;
In keeping Sherlock safe and whole
From mania and depression's toll,
 I was indeed his debtor.

Then, as in chastened thought I sat,
 The clock began to chime.

I rose, collected cane and hat,
Resolving to avoid the flat
    Till some *much* later... time...

Of course, of *course*, what better gift
    Than timepiece ornamental?
I said goodbye; my hostess sniffed,
Though stern expression seemed to lift,
    Her voice in farewell gentle:

"Take care, young man, and give my best
    To happy bride and groom!
But if I might perhaps suggest?
It oft means more to have a guest
    Than *things* to fill a room."

I nodded slowly, stepping out
    Into the bustling street.
Just then, I heard a hailing shout:
"Good heavens! Mycroft, *you're* about
    In all this sweltering heat?"

"Good evening, Sherlock," I replied,
    "And you too, Doctor Watson.
But back to Whitehall I must ride –
May I suggest you go inside,
    Escape this baking hot sun?

"Goodbye, dear ma'am, my humblest thanks!"
    And thus, I calmly went;
The river Thames would burst its banks
Before Sherlock could fill the blanks
    And fathom my intent.

The Doctor, though, I smiled to note,
    Appeared to have a notion.
My brother's gifts, of which he wrote,
At times were a mere rowing boat
    Upon John Watson's ocean.

The Adventure of the Twinkling Hat: A Novella

Readers may have worked out that the rhyme 'Twinkle, Twinkle' refers to 'The Musgrave Ritual'. I wanted to round off this collection of verses by expanding those combined ideas into a new story, taking Holmes and Watson further through the Looking-Glass than they've ever been before...

~0~

One thing was certain, that *Watson* had had nothing to do with it – it was Mrs. Hudson's fault entirely. For the landlady, while astonishingly tolerant of Sherlock Holmes's more eccentric habits (such as keeping cigars in the coal scuttle and transfixing his unanswered correspondence to the mantelpiece with a jack-knife), had finally put her foot down regarding the detective's case files. Holmes refused to destroy documents connected with his past cases, yet he could rarely muster the energy to docket and arrange them. Month after month his papers would accumulate, until every corner of the sitting room was stacked with bundles of manuscript; and Mrs. Hudson had thus announced to both of her lodgers that very morning that she would be taking a well-deserved holiday until the flat was a good deal more habitable.

"And the moral of that, Mr. Holmes," the woman said severely, "is 'Make a mountain *into* a molehill.' You may cable me at the end of the week."

Holmes could scarcely deny the justice of the request, but still thought the landlady's methods deeply underhanded – she'd never have saved up punishments like this for Watson! The detective had sat sulking on the sitting room floor since Mrs. Hudson's departure, surrounded by empty cartons and piles of paper in varying degrees of order, while Watson lounged in his armchair, half asleep, pretending (and failing) to look sympathetic. As the morning wore on, however, with little noticeable progress made, Watson was reluctantly considering an offer of assistance when the doorbell rang.

"I'll go!" Holmes scrambled up and dashed downstairs, while Watson groaned, casting his eyes heavenward – it must be the postboy. Just what they needed: *more* cases to add to these mile-high stacks! So much for having Mrs. Hudson back by Sunday night...

The front door banged shut, and Holmes's returning footsteps sounded on the stairs. "I say, Watson," the detective called, sounding suspiciously cheerful, "have I ever mentioned a man called Reginald Musgrave to you?"

"I... don't believe so," Watson answered cautiously. "Former client of yours?"

Holmes appeared in the doorway with a handful of envelopes, one already opened. "A scion of one of Britain's very oldest families. We were at the same college together; I had some slight acquaintance with him." He dropped onto the settee, carelessly stuffing the remaining post into his jacket pocket. "He wasn't generally popular, but I always thought that what others took for pride was really extreme natural diffidence. He looked every inch an aristocrat, too: thin, large-eyed, high-nosed..." (Watson's lips twitched, but said nothing.) "...with languid but courtly manners."

"Well, if you two had so little in common, why is he writing?" Watson couldn't resist asking, ignoring the scowl from the settee.

"We drifted into talk once or twice," Holmes answered acidly, "and he expressed a keen interest in my methods of observation and inference." Unlike *some* people he could mention. "I've heard nothing of him since graduating, but now it seems he's suddenly taken it into his head to invite the pair of us down to his estate."

"...oh, yes?"

"Indeed," Holmes continued blithely, pretending he hadn't heard the note of resignation. "Hurlstone Manor, a rambling, freezing old pile in West Sussex – you'll find its history fascinating, I'm sure."

"Now, really, Holmes," Watson said sternly, "it's very good of your old schoolfellow to remember you like this, and to invite us both, but this mess is going to take several days to sort through..."

"Oh, a week at least," Holmes grinned, jumping up again. "So do make haste and pack, there's a good chap."

"*Holmes!*" Watson sat bolt upright as the detective escaped to his bedroom, hauling his valise down from the wardrobe. "Don't you dare! You didn't only promise Mrs. Hudson to make the place liveable again, remember, you promised *me!*"

"Contrariwise, Watson," Holmes tossed airily over his shoulder. "In point of fact, you read my brooding silence as a tacit agreement. Besides, I've already sent off an express telegram with the postboy, graciously accepting on both our behalves. Now, what trains shall we need tomorrow..." He rummaged in his bureau drawer for the Bradshaw.

The doctor shook his head weakly, rising and picking his way across the floor through the abandoned piles. "Holmes, you can't be serious. Mrs. Hudson will stand on her head when she sees you've simply left the litter as it is!" If anything, the mess was even worse than before.

"But that's the beauty of it, Watson," Holmes insisted. "She won't return until the job is completed! Thus, the longer we take to do it, the better holiday she'll have!"

We? Watson sighed, then shook his head again much more firmly, arms folded. "*No*, Holmes."

Holmes blinked. "No?"

"You heard me: I'm not going to Sussex, and neither are you. I refuse to be a party to your childish nonsense this time, nohow!"

~0~

"Come, come, my dear fellow," Holmes wheedled, shutting the compartment door and unfolding his newspaper as he sat down. "You can't possibly maintain that charming disposition *all* the way to Sussex." A glowering silence was the only response, and the detective sighed. "You didn't have to come, you know."

"Contrariwise, Holmes," Watson said in a sing-song voice. "In point of fact, I'd wager a thousand pounds that, without me along to pour cold water on your plans for a quick getaway, Mrs. Hudson would have returned to Baker Street out of sheer morbid curiosity long before you did!" (Particularly since Watson would have flatly refused to cable any kind of reassuring lies on Holmes's behalf.)

"Whereas in reality, you allowed yourself to be swayed by the promise of wholesome country air, unbroken nights, a little trout fishing, the finest cook in the county..." Holmes smirked at the faraway look that crept into Watson's eyes. "Not to mention..."

"Yes, yes, all *right!*" Watson reddened, avoiding Holmes's gaze, as irritated with himself as anything else. Holmes knew his flatmate's weaknesses only too well, damn him. An offhand proposal that Watson might read some of his earliest case records upon their return, with perhaps a view to publishing one or two, had simply been too great a temptation to bear.

"Tickets!" came the guard's voice from the corridor.

"Why did the railway have to make the tickets so much larger?" Holmes grumbled as he fished in his breast pocket. "You can barely fit them into a wallet nowadays!"

"Yes," Watson said dryly, producing his own neatly folded in two. "A few more holidays, and Mrs. Hudson could probably repaper the sitting room with them. I don't suppose...?" It would certainly improve domestic relations if the good woman came home to find a plasterer had been in to fix the bullet holes.

"I would sooner jump the Thames with this train," Holmes replied flatly.

The compartment door opened, and the guard put his head in. "Tickets, please!" he snapped breathlessly. Watson couldn't blame him for being out of sorts: the poor fellow's pockets were already stuffed to bursting with oversized ticket halves, so that he appeared at first glance to be dressed in pasteboard.

"My good man," Holmes frowned in genuine concern, "you're practically bent double under those! Here, allow me." And turning the guard around, he pinned their two halves to the shoulders of his coat to better balance him out. "You must buy a coat with pockets in back as soon as you can."

"Much obliged, yer honour!" the guard beamed, and staggered on down the corridor.

Watson could only look on at the exchange in bewilderment. "Holmes," he ventured as the detective shut the door again, "pray don't misunderstand me, I'm sure you meant well..."

Holmes arched an affronted eyebrow. "But?"

"Well, I mean, if those tickets are so *very* heavy..."

"Yes?"

Watson shrugged. "He could class them in future as luggage and use a barrow."

~0~

A wagon and horses stood waiting at the small wayside station where the pair descended. The half-hour drive took them along a broad, white road through a splendid park, and Watson, despite his initial misgivings, felt his spirits lift with every turn of the wheels. He had often observed that autumn seemed to cast a sleepy, almost mournful quality over the countryside; but how beautiful these grand old oaks were, their gilt-edged leaves burnished by the afternoon sun, and how crisp and clean the

September air! Holmes was, for once, perfectly right. They had both been sorely in need of time away from Baker Street, the stacks could wait a few days more.

"There it is, Watson!" Holmes said at last, nudging the doctor out of his reverie. "Hurlstone Manor." And indeed, that 'rambling, freezing old pile' lay before them at the end of a long avenue, surrounded by beautifully landscaped gardens.

"Magnificent!" Watson exclaimed as they rolled onwards. He might once have read a description of the famous old building, but mere words completely failed to do it justice. The house was built in the shape of an L, the short arm clearly the older portion from which the longer, more modern arm had developed. "Look at those tiny windows in the original hall, they must date from the sixteenth century, at least!"

Holmes nodded, smiling at his friend's enthusiasm. "It's thought to be the oldest inhabited building in the county. I can see that you and our host will get on famously, pottering through the venerable wreckage of his feudal keep."

"Doesn't the house's history interest you?"

"Not especially," Holmes shrugged, "but no doubt some form of occupation will present itself in due course." He arched an eyebrow as the doctor frowned. "Really, Watson, what does it matter where my body happens to be? My mind goes on working all the same."

"That's true," Watson sighed, "although I was hoping that this holiday would be a satisfactory one for us both – and by 'satisfactory', I mean an enriching and refreshing time, with no onerous adventures to be embarked upon!"

"That's a lot to make one word mean," Holmes said straight-faced, a faint quiver of laughter in his voice. "Are you paying it for the extra work?"

Watson was too much puzzled to respond, and they were almost at the front door in any case, from which a man in a black suit had just emerged, followed by two footmen. A few moments later, a fourth figure appeared, who precisely matched Holmes's description of their host: thin and large-eyed with a keen, pale face, dressed like a young man of fashion. Something of Reginald Musgrave's birthplace seemed to cling to him, the aristocratic profile and poise of his head irresistibly reminding Watson of grey archways and mullioned windows.

"My dear Holmes," Musgrave smiled, coming forward as the pair climbed down, "what a pleasure to see you again."

"And you, Musgrave," Holmes answered cordially, shaking hands. "My friend and colleague, Dr. Watson."

"Glad you could come, Doctor," Musgrave responded heartily. "I was delighted to learn that Holmes had turned those powers with which he used to amaze us at college to practical ends. And such thrilling accounts you've written of your adventures, one might almost be there oneself!"

"Too kind," Watson murmured, reddening. A sudden cawing in the trees to his right provided an excellent pretext to look away, which was followed an instant later by a *thump* from the wagon: the younger footman had lost his grip on Watson's valise.

"Careful, Dom!" the older footman hissed, while the butler frowned sternly at the luckless youth, who scrambled down, red-faced, and scuttled inside with the case.

"Is your brother quite well?" Holmes asked the older footman, who stiffened in mild surprise.

"Oh, Tweed'll be fine," Musgrave said, sounding more amused than mystified at the detective's ready display of keen observation. "He just doesn't like birds very much, poor fellow, especially the larger sort. I never thought to mention Hurlstone had a community of crows when I engaged the pair, but he puts up with them well enough. Gentlemen, this is Brunton, my butler, and as you correctly deduced, Holmes, *Mister* Tweed, the senior footman."

"I ought to have noticed the resemblance myself," Watson said ruefully as the remaining staff bowed in greeting, giving the older Tweed a kindly nod in return.

"And how has all gone with you, Musgrave?" Holmes asked. "I was sorry to hear of your father's death two years ago."

"Yes, thank you." Musgrave gestured invitingly towards the front door, and the three made their way inside. "Well, they do say work is the best antidote to sorrow. I've had the estate to manage, of course, and I'm now a member for my district."

"You have been busy," Watson smiled. He could only imagine what it took just to keep a house this size in order, Mrs. Hudson would probably throw up her hands in despair. "Do you entertain very much?"

"Mostly shooting parties in the pheasant months," Musgrave said, halting suddenly with an awkward look. "To own the truth, gentlemen... I hope you won't be offended, but your invitation was partly inspired by an acquaintance in the district. I mentioned to Reverend Heyer last week that you and I were schoolfellows, Holmes, and he expressed such delight at the fact that I couldn't resist the chance to surprise him. He's quite old, due for retirement in a few years, and he hasn't much to look forward to besides hearing confessions – and he gets few enough of those in these parts, I daresay." This adjoinder was accompanied by a wry smile, just as the butler entered the hall with the footmen and the last of the bags. (Watson would later remember the odd flicker of emotion in Brunton's eyes at his master's seemingly innocent remark, although his face remained properly impassive.)

"He'll be dining with us this evening, in fact. He's quite a good card player, and if you're not too fatigued, I thought we might get up a game or two after dinner."

"That's an excellent idea," Watson enthused. "What do you think, Holmes... Holmes?"

"Hm?" Holmes blinked, his attention seemingly having been arrested by a nearby suit of armour, a vicious-looking mace clutched in one gauntlet. "Oh, indeed, a splendid idea." Although Watson doubted the detective had actually heard what the idea was at all.

Musgrave shook his head at himself. "Forgive me, gentlemen. Here I am, keeping you standing about, and you must be worn out from the journey. Brunton will show you up to your rooms."

~0~

Watson was pleased to find that his apartment faced south, giving him a lovely view of the avenue and front grounds through diamond-paned windows. The cawing of the crows in the nearby trees was much clearer from up here, but not unpleasant; the doctor had always thought it a solemn, venerable sort of sound, somehow adding to the dignity and grandeur of the place. But the shadows of the great trees were already stealing across the lawn like thieving fingers, and he might easily be late for dinner if he didn't bestir himself to dress.

He was combing his hair in the washstand mirror, when in the reflection he saw a large shadow flicker across the window. Watson didn't think anything of it after the first moment of surprise, but then a sharp tapping on the window made him start, turning around to get a proper look. A crow was standing on the outside ledge, tilting its head to stare into the room with one beady eye, then the other, then resumed pecking on the glass.

Watson sighed, and went over and opened the window, meaning to gently shoo the bird away. But the crow didn't fly off when the pane swung out, merely hopping a little further along the ledge, keeping just out of arm's reach. It seemed to be quite a young one, now that he came to look closely, and Watson couldn't help admiring the handsome picture it made, glossy black plumage gilded by the setting sun, appearing completely unafraid of a mere human. In the same moment, the doctor noticed something glittering in the bird's beak.

"Hullo, what have you got there, my fine fellow?" he asked without thinking, and smiled when the crow *cawed* back at him as if in answer. The object dropped from its beak onto the ledge with a tinkle, and rolled off into the garden below: a farthing!

"Oh dear," Watson frowned, as the crow croaked in dismay at the loss of its treasure. "Hard luck, old chap!" Then an idea struck him. "Wait a moment..." Digging out his purse from his coat pocket, he chose the newest florin he could find, and placed it flat on the ledge. "Here you are, have this one."

The crow left off peering down into the flower bed and cocked its head, giving Watson the most inscrutable sideways look he'd ever gotten from any living creature (including

Holmes). But before either of them could react further, the sound of the dinner gong came from downstairs.

"Bother," Watson murmured, feeling an odd pang of annoyance at the interruption. "Well, good evening," he nodded politely, closed the window, and hastened to complete his toilet.

~0~

Holmes looked up from the foot of the main staircase as Watson came down, arching an inquiring brow at the gleam of amusement in the doctor's eyes. What had the man been up to?

Watson shook his head, smiling foolishly. "Never mind, it's nothing."

"If you'll please to come this way, gentlemen." Brunton had appeared in one of the front hall's numerous doorways. "Mr. Musgrave and Reverend Heyer are in the drawing room."

"Oh, the Reverend's here already?" Watson said, falling in beside Holmes and following the butler along the passage. "I didn't see him arrive."

"No, sir, you likely wouldn't have," Brunton answered, and Holmes could hear a faint note of displeasure in the man's voice. "The Reverend prefers to walk from the vicarage, and the shortest route is by a path and stile on the north side of the park." Which would bring Heyer to the back door, the detective surmised – hence the butler's disapproval.

"As the crow flies, then?" Watson quipped, chuckling at his own wit. "Good for him, we like a clergyman who doesn't stand on ceremony, eh, Holmes?" Holmes was spared from answering by their arrival in the drawing room.

"Good evening, gentlemen, do come in. Refreshed, I hope?" Musgrave left his sherry glass and came forward with the newest arrival, beaming. "Reverend Heyer, allow me to introduce Mr. Sherlock Holmes and Dr. John Watson of London. Gentlemen, the Very Reverend Vicar Marcus Heyer, our long-suffering parish priest."

"It's my very g-great pleasure to m-meet you, sirs," Reverend Heyer stammered. Holmes was intrigued to note that the priest had unusually narrow ears, which were turning as red as a rose while the rest of his face remained pale. "W-Welcome to Hurlstone!"

"Thank you, Reverend," Holmes smiled, bowing, and Watson followed suit. "The pleasure is ours."

"Brunton was just telling us about the church being close by," Watson said. "If it's half as old as the manor, I'd love to pay a visit."

"Oh, yes indeed, d-do come!" Heyer answered enthusiastically, the tip of his long nose quivering. "I sh-should be glad to have you both, there's *plenty* of room!"

There was a polite cough behind them from the butler. "Dinner is served, sirs."

~0~

Contrary to the detective's expectations, dinner passed pleasantly enough. The Tweed brothers were among the staff waiting on them that evening, and Holmes was glad to see that the younger Tweed looked much more composed in his duties.

The food was of course excellent, Watson waxing almost lyrical in his praise of the oyster stew, and Reverend Heyer proved an intelligent conversationalist on a variety of subjects, if a little too fond of conundrums for Holmes's taste. ("A *writing desk?*" Watson blinked, laughing. "I can't imagine!")

After dinner, the company moved to the library, a comfortable firelit room with a well-stocked sideboard. An elderly red setter had been snoozing on the hearthrug, but lifted its head hopefully as the men came in, tail wagging. "Good boy, Rex," Musgrave greeted affectionately, scratching behind the silky ears. "Go back to sleep, old fellow, all's well."

"Hullo, boy," Holmes smiled, and bent to let Rex sniff his hand before gently stroking the dog's greying coat. "Having a well-earned rest, eh?" he murmured, an odd wistfulness suddenly stealing over him. "Dreaming of all those glorious hunting days, long past..." Then he saw that Musgrave was watching with a poorly concealed grin, and straightened hastily, cheeks faintly pink. "What a handsome animal."

"I say, Holmes, come and see this!" Watson called from across the room, and the detective gratefully joined him, followed by their host. The doctor stood with Heyer next to a display case tucked discreetly into one corner, pointing through the glass. "Look, a seventeenth-century broadsword, basket hilt. Family heirloom, Musgrave? It's in splendid condition!"

Musgrave nodded proudly. "Yes, my ancestor, Sir Ralph Musgrave, was a prominent Cavalier – one of Charles the First's strongest supporters, in fact."

"Brandy, sir?"

"Ah, thank you, Brunton. And that document to the left is his commission and seal, signed by Prince Rupert, cavalry commander at the fateful battle of Edgehill."

Brunton cleared his throat again. "If I may make so bold, sir..." The butler seemed oddly animated compared to his earlier air of detachment. "Sir Ralph Musgrave first joined Prince Rupert's cavalry troop at Banbury – five days *after* Edgehill."

"Ah." Holmes's lips twitched as Musgrave flushed. "Did he, indeed. Yes, well, thank you, Brunton, you may leave us now."

"Very good, sir," Brunton replied, expression turning wooden again, but Holmes couldn't help sympathising with the gleam of resentment in the butler's eye. "Good night."

Musgrave laughed awkwardly as the butler left the room, casting himself into a chair and waving the others towards theirs with a regal hand. "Brunton was once a schoolmaster, you know. I often have to bow to his expertise in matters of local history, particularly my own family."

"I see," Watson said thoughtfully, brow slightly furrowed as if he too had been irked by their host's condescension towards a valued retainer.

"Well, gentlemen, join me in a game of cards? I've warned these two you're a famous cardsharp, Reverend," Musgrave joked, "and they're still keen to play."

"S-Splendid," Heyer chuckled, rising, "although I deduce from those admiring looks at the mantel that you prefer ch-chess, Mr. Holmes?"

"I do indeed," Holmes smiled, and got up himself to help set up the card table. "That's a very handsome set you have, Musgrave – it's a shame about the missing piece."

"What?" Musgrave frowned, coming over. Sure enough, one of the red knights was missing. "Oh, I wonder where that went?" A quick hunt around the shelves and floor by all four turned up nothing but another pack of cards, Musgrave even apologetically lifting Rex's paws and the hearthrug, just in case the dog had mistaken the knight for a new toy. "What a nuisance! I'll have to ask the staff about it in the morning. Now then, what shall we play?"

They decided on Hearts, as Watson regretfully admitted that he had no head for whist that evening. During play, the conversation inevitably returned to Musgrave's enigmatic butler, Holmes inquiring how long Brunton had been in service at Hurlstone.

"Twenty years or so. I remember when my father first took him up: a young man of great energy and character, he soon became quite invaluable." Musgrave shook his head with a sigh. "The butler of Hurlstone... Every visitor always remembers that!

He has some extraordinary gifts – he can speak several languages and play any musical instrument – and I've often wondered why he should have been content for so long in such a position."

"Well, I suppose he's been c-comfortable," Reverend Heyer suggested, dealing the next round, "and lacked the energy to m-make any change."

"Mm, perhaps. But this paragon does have one fault. He's a bit of a Don Juan, which isn't a difficult part to play in a quiet country district! It was all right when he was married, but since his poor wife died last year, we've had no end of trouble with him." (Holmes mused sardonically that 'all right' probably meant that Musgrave hadn't personally had to smooth over any domestic scandals until after the funeral.) "A few months ago, we hoped he was about to settle down again, for he became engaged to Rachel Howells, our second housemaid; but he's thrown her over since then and gone after Janet Tregellis, daughter of my head game-keeper. Rachel's a good girl, but rather excitable, and she had a touch of brain fever recently. Goes about the house now like a black-eyed shadow of her former self!"

"Poor girl!" Watson murmured. "Oh, speaking of black-eyed shadows... I had a rather amusing encounter with one of your crows outside my window just before dinner. They do seem marvellously trusting of humans!"

Musgrave chuckled. "A young one, was it? That'd be Jack Tar, then. Mrs. Hart the cook rescued him when he fell out of the nest as a fledgling, and now he seems to think the manor is a massive stone tree!"

Heyer tittered. "Crows are remarkably intelligent b-birds, aren't they?"

"I should say so. Do you know, some experts think they can not only memorise human faces to avoid danger, but then pass that information on to other crows? It's really rather fascinating."

"You seem to be quite the expert yourself, Musgrave," Holmes said innocently. "I wonder you don't write your own monograph."

Musgrave looked faintly flattered, while Watson kicked Holmes's foot under the table, then groaned as he realised he'd been left holding the Queen of Spades – thirteen points!

"Oh, bad luck, Watson!" Holmes commiserated, totalling up the scores while trying not to look smug at having far fewer points than the other three. "Another game, gentlemen?"

~0~

Retiring to his room for the night, Watson remembered Jack Tar and looked along the window ledge – the coin was gone. He hoped the bird had managed to pick that one up without dropping it. The four-poster bed was very comfortable, and Watson quickly fell asleep, plunging into a vivid dreamscape. He saw the uniformed Tweed brothers marching side by side along a beach, a long line of oysters behind them, running to catch up on little legs... and then Rex the red setter was wandering around a large chess board, sniffing at the missing knight's space before curling up in it and going to sleep, snoring as loudly as a steam engine while the other pieces tiptoed carefully around him...

~0~

Watson woke the next morning to find clear skies, but the windows speckled with raindrops. Well, that explained why he'd dreamt of the sea last night – the rain must have been loud enough on the roof to penetrate even his slumber! Holmes and Musgrave were already at breakfast when the doctor came down, neither one looking as if they had spent a very restful night.

"Good morning, Watson."

"Good morning, Doctor. Sleep well?"

"Good morning, gents. Very well, thank you." Watson sat down to his soft-boiled egg and soldiers with a smile of anticipation. "Although this county's air must be stronger than I thought – I had the most peculiar dream..." He tapped the top of his egg with his spoon, and all three jumped the next moment at a resounding *crash* in the passage outside, and a female cry of distress.

"That's Rachel!" Musgrave frowned in concern, scrambling up and following the other two out into the hall, Watson knocking over his eggcup in his haste.

They found the maid kneeling on the rug, trying to gather up a tray of shattered crockery. Rachel Howells looked dreadfully pale, a shawl around her shoulders pinned all on one side – and, of all things, a hairbrush tangled in her hair.

"My dear girl," Watson said gently, "are you hurt?" He and Holmes helped the young woman up and sat her down on a nearby chair, examining her face and trembling hands for cuts.

"You're still not well, Rachel," Musgrave said, kindly but firmly. "You should be resting. Don't come back to your duties until you are stronger."

Rachel gave him a strange, frantic look. "I am strong enough, sir. I'm ever so much be-e-etter!"

"I'll be the judge of that," Watson answered in a voice that brooked no argument; the poor girl's pulse was racing like a thoroughbred's. "You must stop work now, and go back to bed."

"And on your way," Musgrave added, "just say that I wish to see Brunton."

A violent shudder shook the maid from head to foot. "The butler is gone."

Musgrave started. "Gone! Gone where?"

"He is gone. No one has seen him." Rachel's voice rose higher and higher. "He is not in his room. Oh yes, he is gone, he is gone!" She fell to her knees on the fragment-littered carpet with shriek after shriek of laughter.

Musgrave rushed to the nearest bell to summon help, while Watson and Holmes did their best to restrain the hysterical maid without hurting her by wrapping the shawl securely around her arms. The Tweeds soon arrived, and helped to carry Rachel to her room, still screaming and sobbing. Watson called for his medical bag, administering a sedative, and remained in attendance while Musgrave and Holmes made inquiries among the rest of the household.

Brunton's bed hadn't been slept in, and he had apparently been seen by no one since retiring to his room the night before. Holmes noticed whenever he asked that question within Musgrave's hearing, however, that his host looked increasingly uncomfortable. Still, it was difficult to see how the butler might have left the house, as none of the windows or outside doors had been found unfastened this morning. Most of his clothes, his watch, and even his money were in his room, although the black suit he usually wore was missing, along with his hat, scarf, raincoat, and a pair of galoshes. It had been raining last night, but the fresh mud on the doormats and scrapers could unfortunately belong to anyone, some of the staff having already gone in and out to attend to their duties. What, then, had Brunton been doing in the night, and what could have become of him?

The next logical step was to search the interior of the manor, meticulously and in pairs. This was carried out with considerable difficulty, as the place was a veritable maze. Holmes had never seen such a house for getting in the way; he was almost prepared to swear at one point that he and Musgrave had walked out of one room, down a short corridor, and straight back into the same room again. Eventually, though, they managed to eliminate the upper stories, descending a flight of back stairs into the kitchen. Mrs. Hart left off making jam tarts for afternoon tea to put the kettle on, all sympathy at the news of Rachel's breakdown, but she didn't seem surprised by it.

"Poor dear, her head was clean off... I mean, she was clean off her head about that scoundrel! I warned her, I did, sirs; knaves like that don't never mend their ways, I said – ooh, Duchess, you *naughty* girl, get out of it!" The last remark was directed at a tortoiseshell cat, which had just slunk out of the cool room, a crescent-shaped smear of cream across its face that might look just like a broad grin to a fanciful person...

Shaking his head at his own whimsy, Holmes left the servants to finish searching the ground floor, turning his attention to the outside of the manor: lawns, plant beds, gravel paths, but all in vain. Not a single footprint could be seen that could definitively be called Brunton's, and the detective returned to the library with Musgrave in a dour frame of mind. Watson was already there with the tea tray and a plate of small cakes, the doctor taking in Holmes's frustrated countenance with a sympathetic smile, preserving a discreet silence until the pair had refreshed themselves.

As Holmes sipped his tea, his gaze was drawn once more to the chess board on the mantelpiece. That missing piece... which had been followed mere hours later by a missing person. Could it have some significance? But if so, who had removed the Red Knight: Brunton himself, or someone else? And... no, wait, there was a *second* piece missing now! Holmes sprang up and rushed to the fireplace, but his eyes had not deceived him. The detective felt suddenly cold, swiftly followed by a hot flood of anger. Lips compressed, he turned to face Watson and Musgrave, voice steely. "Gentlemen... the White Queen is gone."

The two men looked at him in bewilderment, although Watson was the first to show any sign of understanding. "Dear heavens... you think the missing pieces might be connected with the case?"

"Precisely." Holmes paced the floor, hands clasped behind him, frowning deeply. "And speaking of missing pieces..." He swung around and gave Musgrave a long, pointed stare. "I think our kind host has delayed his confession long enough. Oh, come, come, Musgrave," the detective snorted, cutting short Musgrave's stammering protest, "that wasn't merely shock in your expression when Rachel Howells told you of Brunton's disappearance – it was *guilt*, plain as a pikestaff. You most certainly know something of what happened to your butler last night, even if you were not the last person to see him alive."

"I..." Musgrave swallowed hard, wide-eyed, then sighed deeply, his shoulders sagging. "Yes... You're quite right, Holmes, God knows how. I did see Brunton after we said goodnight, I even spoke with him. But what I don't understand is why he left so suddenly!"

"Then you were at least aware that he meant to leave?"

"Well, I didn't think so at the time, but... what choice did he have?" Musgrave smiled ruefully at Holmes's arched brows. "I'd best start at the beginning, I suppose."

"I can never sleep when it rains, and after struggling to do so until two in the morning, I gave up and lit the candle, intending to continue a novel I was reading. I had left the book in this room, so I pulled on my dressing-gown and came down to get it. As you may remember, I had extinguished the lamp in here and closed the door before coming to bed, so you can imagine my surprise when, as I approached, I saw a glimmer of light coming from the now open door.

"Naturally, my first thought was of burglars. I took a battle-axe from the wall, and then, leaving the candle behind me, I crept down the passage and peeped in at the door. It was Brunton. He was sitting in that very easy chair, fully dressed, with a piece of paper which looked like a map upon his knee, and his forehead sunk forward upon his hand in deep thought. He had a small taper on the card table, shedding a feeble light, while I stood dumb with astonishment, watching him from the darkness. Suddenly he rose, walked to the bureau over there, unlocked it and took a paper from one of the drawers. Returning to his seat, he flattened it out beside the taper, and began to study it intently.

"I felt so indignant at this calm examination of our family documents that I discarded caution and stepped into the room. Brunton looked up and saw me, and sprang to his feet, face livid with fear, thrusting into his breast the paper he'd originally been studying.

" 'So!' I said angrily. 'This is how you repay the trust I have reposed in you. You will leave my service tomorrow.'

"He bowed, looking utterly crushed, and slunk past me without a word. The taper was still on the table, and by its light I glanced to see what the paper was that Brunton had taken from the bureau. To my surprise, it was nothing of any importance at all, simply a copy of the questions and answers in the singular old observance called the Musgrave Ritual." Musgrave smiled faintly at the twin intrigued expressions of his audience. "It's a sort of ceremony peculiar to our family. Every Musgrave has gone through it on his coming of age for centuries. It might be of some interest to an archaeologist, I suppose, but no practical use."

Holmes hummed reservedly, rubbing his chin. "We'd better come back to the paper afterwards."

"All right... Anyhow, I relocked the bureau, turned to go, and started on seeing that Brunton had returned, standing in front of me.

" 'Mr. Musgrave, sir,' he cried hoarsely, 'I can't bear disgrace, sir. I've always been proud above my station in life, and disgrace would kill me. My blood will be on your head, sir – it will, indeed – if you drive me to despair. If you cannot keep me after what has passed, then for God's sake let me give you notice and leave in a month, as of my own free will. I could stand that, Mr. Musgrave, but not to be cast out before all the folk that I know so well.'

" 'You don't deserve much consideration, Brunton,' I answered. 'Your conduct has been infamous. However, you have served my family well for many years, and I have no wish to bring public disgrace upon you. You may take yourself away in a week, and give what reason you like for going.'

" 'Only a week, sir?' he cried in a despairing voice. 'Say at least a fortnight!'

" 'A week,' I repeated firmly, 'and you may consider yourself to have been very leniently dealt with.' He crept away, head bowed, while I put out the light and returned to my room."

~0~

Musgrave gratefully accepted a second cup of tea from Watson, throat becoming dry from his recital. "I won't deny that, on reflection, I was somewhat glad Brunton had bargained for more time. After all, it wouldn't have done to be shorthanded with guests in the house. But *why* would he then have disappeared overnight, after begging me for a month's grace?"

"I suspect the answer lies in that paper, Musgrave," Holmes said, "which your butler thought worth his while to consult, even at the risk of losing his place. May we see it?"

"Yes, of course." Musgrave unlocked the bureau again and brought a large, yellowing roll of parchment to the table. "It is rather an absurd business, this ritual of ours, but it has antiquity to excuse it, at least. The document is undated, but Reverend Heyer believes the spelling is mid-seventeenth century."

"The Reverend has seen it, too?" Watson asked, frowning.

"Well, yes – on the same day I had the thought to invite the pair of you, actually. Heyer was paying his customary Saturday afternoon visit, and the conversation drifted around to a treatise he's writing on local customs and traditions. He was most intrigued by this particular one, although he couldn't make it out any better than the rest of us. 'A m-mystery worthy of the great Sherlock Holmes,' he said. 'Well, it's funny you should say that,' I answered..."

Holmes sighed, forbearing to comment. "Was Brunton in the room at any point during your discussion of the Ritual?"

"He... could have been? If so, I might easily have missed him!" Musgrave shrugged, flushing defensively. "That's the mark of a good servant, though, isn't it? You don't notice them unless you need them."

Holmes could hardly deny the truth of that, however much he disliked it, while Watson on the other side of the table was visibly refraining from making any unconstructive comments. "And he had probably seen this document many times before that afternoon, given his long service."

"It's very possible. We took no pains to hide it."

"Then I should imagine that Brunton was refreshing his memory last night."

"But what *could* he want with this old family custom of ours?" Musgrave unrolled the document, Watson and Holmes bending over it. A pair of crests came into view first (the Musgrave and the English coats of arms), followed by the text, which had been penned in a graceful calligraphic hand, and was surrounded by a number of fanciful illuminations. "It doesn't seem to me to be of any practical importance at all."

"Well, Brunton appears to have taken the opposite view, at least," Holmes remarked, his eye drawn from the text by some of the illustrations. Musgrave's ancestors clearly hadn't been immune to the modern craze for all things medieval, either. One of the creatures was so stylised he couldn't even make it out – was that a white mouse, or a rabbit? "This is a very strange catechism, though." He returned to his seat, leaning back with fingers steepled. "Would you and Watson be so kind as to read it out?"

Watson cleared his throat, peering at the elegant script. " 'Whose was it?' "

" 'His who is gone.' " Musgrave wasn't even bothering to read, answering confidently from memory.

" 'Who shall have it?' "

" 'He who will come.' "

" 'What was the month?' "

" 'The sixth from the first.' "

" 'Where was the sun?' "

" 'Over the oak.' "

" 'Where was the shadow?' "

" 'Under the elm.' "

" 'How was it stepped?' "

" 'North by ten and by ten, east by five and by five, south by two and by two, west by one and by one, and so under.' "

" 'What shall we give for it?' "

" 'All that is ours.' "

" 'Why should we give it?' "

" 'For the sake of the trust.' " Musgrave bowed slightly to Watson's expression of admiration, which rapidly became one of bewilderment. "Well, what do you make of it, Doctor?"

Watson laughed despairingly. "I think you might as well read it in a mirror, for all the sense it makes! It's even worse than one of Reverend Heyer's conundrums!" He hesitated. "I don't suppose either of you..."

"*No*, Watson, I haven't the least idea of why a raven is like a writing desk. Do please concentrate on the task at hand, my dear fellow." Then it dawned on Holmes, as he looked back at the ritual document, that Watson had just said something extremely pertinent... "One moment." He picked up the manuscript and carried it over to the fireplace, where a large mirror hung over the mantelpiece. "Now, gentlemen, observe. One might not be able to read the *text* back to front..." Holmes held the top of the document up to the mirror. "But if we reverse this crest..."

"Then the English coat of arms becomes the Scottish," Musgrave shrugged. "What about it?"

"Well, not quite, but near enough." The Scottish unicorn and English lion supporting the shield had switched places, while the golden lilies and lions in the top half had changed places with the red rampant lion.

"The Lion and the Unicorn were fighting for the crown..." Watson recited absently.

"Precisely, Doctor. That heraldic combination of lion and unicorn dates all the way back to 1603, when James the Sixth was crowned James the First of England."

"Indeed," Holmes said thoughtfully. "Your family has a strong connection to the Stuart bloodline, Musgrave. And if you will excuse my saying so, your butler appears to have been a very clever man. I suspect that when Heyer last visited you, Brunton either saw or overheard something which gave him fresh insight into the Ritual's meaning – or so he believed. You mentioned he had some sort of map or chart which he was comparing with the manuscript? A chart by its very nature suggests an object of some kind, waiting to be discovered. Thus, Brunton must have thought there was something of value to be gained, a secret which had escaped ten generations of country squires."

Musgrave gaped. "Well! ...What do you think it was, then?"

"I should prefer not to speculate just now... but these measurements in the Ritual must refer to some spot to which the rest of the document alludes. If we can find that spot, we should be in a fair way towards determining Brunton's fate, at the very least."

"And we already have two guides," Watson said excitedly, glancing back over the parchment. "An oak tree and an elm..." Then he stopped smiling as Musgrave's face fell. "What is it?"

"Oh, the oak's there, all right, Doctor," Musgrave sighed, "a very patriarch among oaks, it might have been there during the Norman Conquest, for all I know! It's the elm, you see... The only one in the garden old enough to have been known to my ancestors was struck by lightning ten years ago."

~0~

Before leaving the house again, Musgrave took Holmes's advice and stationed the Tweeds outside Rachel Howells's room. Watson had sent word to the local doctor for a nurse to watch over the sedated young woman, but Holmes was leaving nothing to chance; he hadn't collected any data thus far to rule out the idea that the second missing chess piece might refer to Rachel. Once the guards had been posted, the trio were free to move on to the next line of inquiry: the Musgrave oak.

Watson had never seen such a magnificent tree, which stood in front of the manor upon the left-hand side of the drive. The only reason he hadn't noticed it on arrival, he concluded, was his enthrallment with the house itself. "I can see why your ancestors chose this as a marker, Musgrave – it must be twenty feet around, at least!"

"Twenty-three at last measurement," Musgrave smiled, placing an affectionate hand on the bulging trunk. "When I was a lad, I used to call it 'the Tum-tum tree' – its trunk looked so like an enormous stomach."

"Fascinating," Holmes murmured sardonically, grey gaze impatiently sweeping the rest of the grounds. "But where did the elm stand?"

"Just over... there." Musgrave faltered as he pointed, as well he might. Watson could now see the scar in the lawn where the elm's stump had been uprooted, nearly midway between the oak and the house. Beside that scar, a long, thin stake appeared to have been hammered into the ground, and perched on the top...

"Isn't that Jack Tar?" Watson asked Musgrave, shading his eyes against the midmorning sun.

"I do believe it is." The crow in question *cawed* loudly as the trio approached, fixing them with one black eye, then flew off towards the manor and perched on the nearest chimney stack.

"Curious..." Watson heard Holmes murmur, then the detective shook his head, returning to practicalities. "It looks as if Brunton *did* come out here last night, and was using the stake as some kind of marker. And this bent nail at the top must have been to hang something: a lantern, most likely. I suppose it's impossible to find out how high the elm was?"

"I can tell you that at once: it was sixty-four feet." Musgrave grinned at Holmes's look of surprise. "When my old tutor taught me trigonometry, it always took the shape of measuring heights. I must have worked out every tree and building on the estate."

"Well, that's a piece of luck!" Watson laughed, then sobered as he realised: if that data had been free for the asking all this time... "Did Brunton ever ask you that?"

Musgrave blinked. "Yes, now that you mention it! He asked me the day before you arrived, almost on this very spot! Said he'd been having an argument with the groom about it. And then..."

"What is it?"

"Well, I've just remembered, he... seemed to be looking at something behind me... and he was smiling."

Holmes's eyes gleamed with intrigue. "As if he had just understood something, perhaps?"

"It's possible... I did turn around and look myself, just out of curiosity, but I couldn't see anything that stood out."

Holmes rubbed his hands together gleefully. "This is excellent news, Musgrave! We *must* be on the right road if we're asking the same questions as Brunton! Now then..." He fished a folded paper out of his pocket, which held a hastily scribbled copy of the Ritual, and consulted it. " 'Where was the sun? Over the oak.' "

"That's rather a vague direction, Holmes," Watson pointed out. " 'Sun over the oak' could mean almost anything if we don't know where to be watching from!"

"Ah, but we do, Watson! 'Where was the shadow? Under the elm.' If there was another position from which to observe the sun, it too would have been mentioned in the Ritual." Holmes pointed to the oak. "When the sun lies over the oak from this vantage point – late afternoon, I should say – the stake's shadow will lie in the same direction as the shadow of the elm would have done. And the Ritual must mean the farther end of the shadow, or the trunk would have been chosen as the guide."

Musgrave nodded. "So, now we have to determine where the far end of the shadow would have fallen... But how are we meant to do that? We can't raise a sixty-four-foot pole... can we?"

Holmes snorted. "Oh, come now, Musgrave! Don't tell me you've forgotten everything your old tutor taught you! Observe this measuring stick which Brunton so kindly left for us. How tall would you say it was, at a glance: four feet?"

"Yes, that seems about right."

"Thus, when we come to measure how much longer its shadow is at the right moment – say, for example, it was six feet (or one and a half times the height) – the calculation for a sixty-four-foot tree ought to be a simple one. Now, all we need are some wooden pegs and a long length of cord..." Holmes started off back towards the house with Musgrave. "Come along, Watson!"

But Watson barely heard him, gazing at the stake Brunton had left behind with a deep sinking feeling. "Holmes... The plan won't work."

Holmes stopped dead, turning to stare at Watson with an almost comical look of surprise. "What? Don't be ridiculous, Watson, of course it will work! It's my own invention, you know."

"No, it won't, Holmes – for *two* very simple reasons." Watson decided not to point out that the detective was actually building on their quarry's ideas, and took the paper from his hand. " 'What was the month? The sixth from the first.' That would mean the seventh month, yes? July? And what month is it now?"

Holmes turned a sickly grey. "September..."

"Exactly. How on earth do you plan to work out where the elm's shadow would have ended if you don't know *precisely* at what height the sun would have been above the oak two months ago? A fraction too low or too high, and the shadow's length could be out by as much as several feet!" Watson put a kindly hand on the crestfallen detective's shoulder. "And even if it were the right month, that wouldn't solve the problem of our being in the wrong century!"

"I'm afraid I don't quite follow, Doctor," Musgrave ventured, though looking just as forlorn as Holmes as the truth of Watson's argument sank in.

"He's right, Musgrave," Holmes groaned, smacking himself on the forehead. "Fool that I am! That blasted Ritual was written two hundred years ago... Even if the oak had stopped growing by then, how much shorter must the elm have been? Whatever measurement we might have taken back in July, the shadow would *still* have been far too long!"

"...ah. Yes, that... might be something of an obstacle..." Musgrave still looked unconvinced, looking thoughtfully at the stake himself, then back across the lawn to the manor. "But, then, wouldn't Brunton have had to solve the same problem? You know, I'm really starting to think he saw *something* that day which helped him get past this point..."

"It wasn't Jack Tar perched on the chimney, by any chance?" Watson joked.

"Watson!" Holmes gasped. "That's it! Callooh! Callay!" he chortled in joy, while the other two looked on in astonishment. The detective dug in his coat pocket for a pencil, snatched the Ritual paper back from Watson and began hastily sketching a series of lines on it, using his knee as a writing desk. "Oh, Brunton, Brunton, you cunning fellow!"

"What, do you mean to say the *crow*...?"

"No, Watson, the house! That is to say, one specific part of the house. Look!" Holmes turned his back directly to the oak, pulled the stake from the ground, and held it straight out in front of him, pointing across the lawn. "Come stand behind me, both of you. Now, what do you see?"

"Only the old wing of the manor," Musgrave began slowly, peering along the stake.

"Exactly!" Holmes crowed, turning and brandishing the paper in front of his colleagues' faces. "*That's* what Brunton saw two evenings ago, Musgrave: *your shadow*, pointing towards the original manor. Your ancestors must have known the elm might grow taller before the secret was uncovered, of course they must! That didn't matter, because the elm's shadow would still point in the right direction whenever the sun was above the oak, no matter how long it was!"

"Good heavens..." Musgrave started to chuckle silently, shaking his head.

Growing tired of the paper flapping in his face, Watson took it from Holmes again and examined the detective's rough sketch.

It didn't seem to make much sense at first: a long upwards arrow, joined at the top by a shorter one pointing right, an even shorter arrow pointing down, and a tiny arrow pointing left, almost looking like a rough spiral...

" 'How was it stepped?' " Holmes's voice murmured excitedly in the doctor's ear.

Watson re-examined the text. " 'North by ten and by ten, east by five and by five... Oh!"

Holmes grinned appreciatively at his friend's reaction. "And I don't know about you, Watson, but I can see only one thing in this vicinity with such a precisely oblong shape..."

Watson closed his eyes. "Of course," he breathed. "Musgrave, these longer arrows may very well represent a partial outline of the old manor's northern end!" The building itself was both map and compass – fiendishly clever! "Are there any doors close to that northeast corner?"

~0~

It was the work of a minute for Holmes to count twenty paces back along the manor wall from the northwest corner, which, as he had already deduced, brought him almost directly in line with the oak and the stake. Now he knew why Brunton had hung a lantern on the stake last night: to see the vanished elm's former position in the dark and rain, and to make doubly certain of which way the tree's shadow would have fallen. Returning to the corner, he carefully paced ten steps east along the north wall, which brought him to the northeast corner. ("We've really got to hope 'by ten and by ten' *does* mean adding rather than multiplying," Musgrave joked, "or we'll be tripping over tree roots out in the park!" Holmes didn't deign to reply.)

Four paces to the south, and the trio were standing before an old oak door, which was locked. "Holmes, are you sure Brunton came this way?" Watson said. "I hate to say it, but this door looks as if it hasn't been opened in years."

"It hasn't," Holmes muttered half to himself, closely examining the lock side. "Look, there's a strand of spider web inside the keyhole. But if the butler knew the house as intimately as I think he must have, he wouldn't need to force his way through here – not when he could reach the far side of the door by an alternate route."

~0~

"Why was this part of the house not searched earlier?" Holmes frowned as Musgrave unlocked the connecting door.

"We only ever use the old wing as a storehouse now. Besides, the door was locked, the other servants would hardly have thought Brunton had locked himself in!"

"I suppose not," Holmes nodded reluctantly, "especially with the key hanging in its usual place. Hullo!" The detective darted forward and bent to examine the stone-flagged floor just inside the door, holding a lantern low. "See here: a fresh smear of mud. This could easily have come from Brunton's galoshes." And now for the outer door!

But when they made their way to the far end of the hall, Holmes felt a cold chill of disappointment. The old, footworn stones in the passage floor were firmly cemented together, and had certainly not been moved recently. The trio got down upon

99

hands and knees, tapping the stones and examining the mortar between, but it sounded the same all over, and there was no sign of any cracks or crevices.

"It's no use, Holmes," Watson sighed, sitting back on his heels. "Brunton couldn't have been at work here!"

"No," Holmes muttered angrily. Where had he gone wrong *this* time? He'd been so certain 'and so under' meant they were to dig!

He didn't realise he'd been speaking aloud until Musgrave answered him: "Well, maybe it means the cellar?"

Holmes lifted his head slowly to stare at the man. "Cellar?"

"Yes, it must be right under this floor." Musgrave flashed him a sheepish grin. "The stairs are through that doorway there."

Resisting the strong impulse to say something he'd regret later, Holmes took a deep breath and rose to his feet, bringing the lantern with him. Sure enough, a winding stone stair lay beyond, ending in a cellar room which had lately been used to store firewood; the billets were scattered over most of the floor, except in the middle. In this cleared space lay a large flagstone with a rusted iron ring set into the centre, to which a thick shepherd's-check muffler was attached.

"By Jove!" Musgrave cried. "That's Brunton's muffler, I could swear to it. What's the villain been doing here?"

"Well, obviously something that required both hands," Watson remarked, "judging by the lantern he left on the floor over there. Looks like it's burned itself out..." The doctor trailed off, his troubled expression matching the other two as a horrible suspicion took hold: what if Brunton hadn't left it behind at all?

"...Come, gentlemen," Holmes said at last, his voice sounding far too hoarse in the dusty silence for his liking. That heavy stone slab was looking more sinister and more smug every moment. "There's no good to be served by delaying."

~0~

With the combined efforts of all three men, the flagstone was lifted and slowly dragged to one side. A black hole yawned beneath, into which Holmes lowered the lantern, revealing a small chamber about seven feet deep and five feet square. At one side of it was a squat, brass-bound wooden box, the lid of which was open, and appeared at first glance to be empty. None of the trio had much thought for the chest at that moment, however, all eyes riveted upon the figure crouched beside it: a man in a black suit, overcoat and galoshes, squatted down on his hams with his forehead resting on the edge of the box and his arms thrown out on each side. The face was hidden, but the corpse's height, dress and hair colour were enough to identify him as the missing butler.

"Dear God..." Musgrave murmured in dismay. "Poor devil! But how on earth did he become trapped down here? He couldn't have lifted that stone by himself, surely – it took all three of us just now!"

"Exactly," Holmes said grimly. "Watson, my dear fellow, would you be so kind?" There was barely room for one other in that space, and he would prefer not to move the body until they'd examined it and the scene together.

Watson nodded in resignation, climbing down carefully and accepting the lantern. "Well, I should say he's been dead for approximately... ten hours? His position has been drawing the stagnant blood to his face, it's beginning to distort the features. Hm, I'm not finding any obvious wounds... or any bruising, either. It looks as if he simply suffocated. And see here..." He moved the lantern nearer to one of Brunton's hands, where the bloodied fingertips and broken nails told their own story. "That stone would have been like a cork in a bottle, he'd have run out of air inside ten minutes."

Musgrave shivered in sympathy. "What a ghastly way to go!"

"Then he must still have been conscious when he was trapped, if he made such a concentrated effort to escape from under it," Holmes mused, not at all keen to try turning the stone over to look for fresh bloodstains. "What does he have in his pockets?"

Watson duly searched. "The usual so far: matches, handkerchief, penknife – oh, that's rather a nice one..."

"His breast pocket, Watson!" Holmes said impatiently. "That chart Musgrave saw him consulting last night should give us at least a little more data."

"Here it is." Watson fished out the paper and unfolded it. "Well, that's odd..."

"What?"

"It's a map all right, but... Here, see for yourself." Watson handed up the paper and the lantern. "It hardly looks like Brunton sketched it in a spare moment, does it?"

"No..." Although the quality of the paper was ordinary foolscap, this drawing of the estate was almost of a professional standard. "It looks rather like Brunton has copied this directly from a blueprint." And where could the butler get his hands on something like that? "Where are the estate archives kept?"

"Well, some of them are kept here, like Sir Ralph's commission," Musgrave said, "and the rest, I suppose, would be at the church with the other parish records."

"Then visiting Reverend Heyer should probably be our next move," Holmes nodded, "once we've finished here." They had indeed thrown a light upon Brunton's fate, but how had that fate come upon him, and what part had been played by his confederate? For Brunton had clearly discovered, just as they had, that the stone was far too heavy for one man to move unaided. What would he do next? He could not get help from outside at that time of night without considerable risk. Far better to have his helpmate from inside the house, but whom could he ask? Rachel Howells, perhaps? A girl of fiery Welsh blood, she had at one time been devoted to him. Had he tried to make his peace with her, engaged her as his accomplice?

"But raising that stone would have been heavy work for just the two of them," Watson exclaimed when Holmes had outlined his theory, "and with Rachel still recovering from her illness! What about his new paramour, Miss... Alice, did you say, Musgrave?"

"No, Tregellis, Janet Tregellis. No, that wouldn't do, she lives with her father on the east side of the wood. I doubt she'd have the nerve for something like this, anyhow!"

"And if we examine some of the nearby billets," Holmes replied, "I think we may find... ah, see here! Several of these pieces are flattened at the sides, as if they've been compressed by a great weight. As the pair dragged the stone up, they must have thrust them into the chink, till at last..." He picked up a billet about three feet long, with a deep groove at one end. "They held the stone up with this once the opening was large enough."

"So Brunton climbed in, opened the box..." Musgrave shivered, eyeing the massive stone uneasily. "Well, that would certainly explain Rachel's hysterics this morning! D'you think, perhaps, she...?"

"I think it would be a mistake to theorise further until we've questioned the girl herself," Holmes said firmly. The detective wished he didn't have such a vivid mental picture of Rachel's hand dashing the support away, the slab crashing back down into its place, the maid then flying wildly up the winding stair, her faithless lover's muffled screams and drumming hands ringing in her ears... "...It may very well be that the wood simply slipped, and Rachel Howells is merely guilty of silence. Now, let us proceed to the chest."

Brunton's stiffened corpse was lifted out of the hole with due care and laid to one side; the cellar was chilly enough to serve as a temporary morgue until the police could be summoned. Watson then gladly switched places with Holmes, as the box couldn't be raised without the risk of it falling to bits. Damp and worms had eaten through the wood, and a crop of mushrooms was growing inside. The only other contents, now that Holmes was close enough to inspect properly, were a couple of old coins, so heavily corroded that they'd been all but invisible at the bottom of the chest. The detective carefully polished one of them on his coat sleeve, and the black coating began to change to a dirty silver, a distinctive profile emerging from the tarnish.

"These are coins of Charles the First!" Holmes called up excitedly. "I was right about your family's connections, Musgrave: they have been safeguarding something of considerable value!"

" 'For the sake of the trust,' " Watson quoted thoughtfully. "But was it only money, do you think, or something more?"

"Really, Watson," Holmes tutted, "can you imagine even a loyal Cavalier swearing to give 'all that is ours' for a bag of silver? This chest most certainly held something other than money." And now there was probably only one living person who knew what the treasure was, or what had become of it... and confound it, they were lying in a drugged stupor upstairs.

With the discovery of Brunton's body, the three now had little choice but to involve the local constabulary. Holmes was confident, however, that his own renown and Musgrave's standing in the community would excuse their disturbing the scene before the police arrived. Musgrave relocked the connecting door to the old wing, marvelling at Rachel's presence of mind in locking the door after herself and replacing the key. Watson then made himself unpopular with the other two by refusing point blank to let them search Rachel's bedchamber for evidence before she was in a fit state to be moved or to answer any questions.

"I am sorry, Holmes, but your curiosity does *not* constitute an actual emergency. It's just as you said, we still don't know for certain if Rachel was involved. Even if she was, she could hardly get far in her condition, and nothing is going to bring Brunton back in any case. I would be remiss in my duty as a physician if I allowed you to endanger a patient's health further by interrogating them or tearing their room apart, all for the want of a little patience!"

Holmes scowled, but he had trapped himself, and he knew it. "Fine," he muttered. "The manor records next, then."

~0~

In other circumstances, Watson would have greatly enjoyed walking through the park with Holmes, Musgrave having elected to wait at the house for the police. The well-worn path wound gently among the trees, the estate's trout pool just visible to their right amid the thick growth; the doctor idly hoped he'd still have a chance to do some fishing before their holiday ended.

Holmes walked in silence most of the way, apparently deep in thought, until they reached the stile of which Brunton had spoken. "An interesting choice, the Red Knight," he remarked suddenly, "don't you think, Watson?"

"Eh?" Watson blinked, pausing with his foot on the step.

"I mean the Red Knight seemingly being used to represent Brunton. Why not choose the White King instead?"

"Given that the White Queen most likely points to Rachel? Yes, it... does seem a little odd, now that you mention it."

"Which gives us a unique opportunity to determine the reasoning of the person responsible, and their identity!" Holmes said excitedly. "Let's begin with the most obvious symbolism: when playing chess, what are the Red Knight and White Queen to each other?"

"Enemies," Watson answered promptly. "The Knight is an invader, bent on entering White territory and, under normal circumstances, capturing the King..."

"Or in this case, perhaps, a treasure *belonging* to royalty," Holmes interjected.

"I suppose that would make Musgrave one of the White Knights, then: a cavalier's descendants guarding the treasure for centuries," Watson mused. "Or maybe the White King, given that he's the highest ranking nobility in these parts?"

"Perhaps... although without any other pieces being moved, we can only speculate there. But what intrigues me most, Watson, is the timing. When did the Red Knight go missing?"

"Last ni... I mean, *at some time* before we were about to play cards last night."

Holmes grinned a 'well done' for spotting the trap. "Yes, it could have been taken at almost any time before that. But think, Watson! It's true that the Knight was noticed missing on the very evening that Musgrave discovered Brunton with the Ritual document. But no one, not even Brunton, could possibly have known *then* that the butler was after the Musgrave treasure, *and* about to be dismissed from Hurlstone!"

"So whatever the Knight's meaning," Watson nodded slowly, "it can't have had anything to do with that dismissal! And as far as we could discover, the only person who had any notion of Brunton's disappearing at all by that time was himself."

"Indeed. I believe Brunton intended the gesture as a sly thumbing of the nose towards his employer, certain as he must have been that he was on the verge of finding the treasure, and making away with it undetected!"

"And Rachel, too, it seems... but then why didn't Brunton remove the Queen at the same time as the Knight, if they were going to leave together?"

"Most likely because he didn't yet know if she *would* escape with him, or even if she was physically strong enough. Once he was certain of her, he could easily have gone back and removed the Queen, before returning to the cellar with Rachel. Besides, two pieces going missing at once might have aroused Musgrave's suspicions."

"Whereas one going missing at first merely looked like an accident, leaving Brunton time to act."

"Exactly." Holmes clapped his friend cheerfully on the shoulder. "Come, Watson, you must admit it's the only explanation that fits all the facts!"

"I suppose so," Watson murmured. Was it his imagination, or did the detective seem a little too relieved at having reached a halfway plausible conclusion? But if Holmes was right, at least that would mean Rachel was in no danger now from an unknown enemy. "I wonder what Brunton did with the pieces..."

~0~

Climbing the stile, the pair came out of the woods to find themselves at the edge of a narrow road. Across from them stood a small church of grey stone with a slated roof, a walled cemetery separating it from a neat little cottage further along the road.

Watson smiled at the picturesque scene, then looked around at a nudge from Holmes's elbow: somebody had just rounded the bend in the road. "Reverend Heyer?" The slight build and wavy white hair were a dead giveaway, even at this distance.

"It *seems* to be," Holmes said in puzzled tones, as well he might. "Is he... dancing?" The man was bobbing up and down, and wriggling like an eel!

Watson snorted at the absurd sight. "No, it looks like he's fishing around in his collar. Something must have gone down his neck. I hope it wasn't a bee!"

Holmes winced at the thought. "Let's go and see if he needs help."

By the time they reached him, however, Heyer had pragmatically pulled the front of his shirt loose and shaken the tiny prisoner free, beaming and pointing into his cupped hand as the pair approached. "L-Look, gentlemen, j-just look! I-It's extraordinary!" A green caterpillar with yellow stripes was inching across the priest's palm, seemingly none the worse for its experience. "An Adonis B-Blue larva, of all things! Who w-would have th-thought it?"

"Who indeed," Holmes murmured, shooting a questioning look at Watson, who shrugged. "I remember you mentioned an interest in entomology last night, Reverend. I gather this is something of a rare find?" The priest's stammer was certainly much more pronounced, Watson noted, which seemed to happen whenever he became excited.

"My dear M-Mr. Holmes!" Heyer chuckled, shaking his head. He spied a nearby patch of cornflowers and daintily placed the caterpillar among them. "The Adonis B-Blue is one of England's rarest b-blue butterflies! And to f-find a larva this late in the s-season, in such a fashion? The ch-chances against it are a-astronomical! I must write to the S-Society at once. Y-You wouldn't object to bearing witness to the d-discovery, I trust?"

"Regrettably, Reverend," Holmes interjected, "we must ask you to set aside your enthusiasm briefly. Mr. Musgrave sends his regards, by the way. He was detained by some urgent estate business – a boundary dispute with one of your other neighbours – and we've come on his behalf to see if there are any maps of the grounds in the parish records. I'm afraid there was nothing of the sort among the manor archives."

"Oh!" Heyer's face fell for a moment as he realised this wasn't merely a social call, then brightened again. "Y-yes, of course, do f-follow me! I keep most of those b-boxes in the vestry..."

"We're not going to tell him about Brunton?" Watson murmured, slowing his steps along with Holmes for a moment as the priest strode eagerly ahead, his loose shirt tail flapping unheeded. Appearances could deceive, of course, but Watson still couldn't imagine anyone less worldly than the Very Reverend

Vicar Marcus Heyer – it was unthinkable that the butler would have enlisted *him* as a willing accomplice on a treasure hunt!

"Not yet," Holmes murmured back, gleaming grey eyes giving nothing away.

~0~

With the reverend's assistance, a search of the most likely boxes did result in some old maps of the entire county, which of course included the location of the estate, but nothing that even vaguely resembled Brunton's paper. Heyer, who had mercifully failed to inquire just which of Musgrave's other neighbours would have need of such a document, expressed his sincere regrets and invited the pair to lunch with him at the vicarage before returning to the manor. "I'm sure M-Miss Hatfield has catered w-well enough for two more."

"Your housekeeper?" Holmes asked, as they strolled through the churchyard towards the wicket gate.

"N-No, the charwoman – I'm only one of the m-many she 'does for' in these parts, bless her," Heyer chuckled. "I believe sh-she even helps Mrs. White on w-wash days at the manor!"

Holmes pricked up his ears at that! Musgrave's laundress... just one of the many servants at Hurlstone besides Brunton who spent a large portion of their days being overlooked by anyone of 'importance'. How many secrets might a charwoman be privy to, with someone like Mrs. White as confidant?

But when they reached the cottage, the small, mousy woman who greeted them swiftly eliminated herself as a suspect. Once Miss Hatfield had been introduced to the guests, and invited to partake herself of the luncheon she'd prepared, she was soon treating Watson's sympathetic ear to a long string of complaints. Most were relatively minor, but of particular interest to Holmes was the lumbago which had apparently laid the woman up at home for the last week. Watson caught the detective's expression, and gave him a sympathetic but firm nod: Miss Hatfield was telling the truth, she knew nothing of the matter. Holmes manfully swallowed his disappointment, and accepted a second slice of plum cake.

"More tea, Doctor?" Miss Hatfield asked, lifting the urn invitingly.

"I haven't had any yet," Watson smiled, "so I can't really take more. But I should like a drop, thank you."

Well, he could hardly take *less*, Holmes mused as he sipped his own cup. A curious blend, this; he could detect notes of chamomile, elderflower, cherry, *pineapple, roast turkey, hot buttered toast...*

~0~

"Holmes? Holmes!" The detective started, and Watson only just caught his tipping cup and saucer before he could be splashed. Poor Holmes looked as mortified as Watson over the slip, not to mention heavy-eyed. "My dear fellow, you're done in!" Watson murmured, chiding himself for not observing his friend's exhausted state earlier, then rose and bowed to their concerned hosts. "Reverend, Miss Hatfield. You've been most hospitable, but we really must take our leave. Musgrave will be wondering what's become of us."

"Y-Yes, of course." Heyer stood and shook hands, although looking oddly at Holmes levering himself up out of his chair. "Please d-do come back and visit wh-whenever you like – I still haven't sh-shown you around the church yet!"

"Thank you, that would be lovely. Good afternoon, Miss Hatfield, it was a pleasure to meet you." Watson carefully steered the almost sleepwalking Holmes outside, across the road and along the woodland path. "I'm terribly sorry, old chap, I ought to have remembered you'd gotten so little rest last night. Let's get you home to bed."

"Home..." Holmes mumbled, smiling dreamily up at the dappled sunlight shining through the leaves. "Home to Hurlstone... I love my love with an H because he is... helpful..."

Watson snorted. "Try 'hilarious'!" How on earth was he going to get Holmes over the stile like this? "I hate y... him with an H because he is hare-brained," he added, deciding not to break whatever spell his friend appeared to be under for the moment. "His name is Holmes –"

"No, *Heyer!*" the detective insisted owlishly. "He lives at Hurlstone... and I fed him with... with..."

"Humbugs and horseradish?" Watson ended with a grin. "Sounds delicious." If he ever obtained permission from Holmes to publish *this* case, he'd need to alter a great many more details than usual!

~0~

Holmes sat at Musgrave's dining table that evening, chin in his hands. There were places enough for well on fifty people, he noted idly, but the only seated guests besides himself appeared to be Miss Hatfield on his left, wearing an enormous flowered bonnet, and a human-sized white rabbit in a waistcoat to his right, a bright blue butterfly pinned to the centre of its clerical collar by way of a bow tie.

"What m-month is it?" the Rabbit asked; it had taken a watch out of its waistcoat pocket and was looking at it anxiously.

"The fourth from the fifth," Holmes replied sadly.

"Two months wrong!" Miss Hatfield sighed. "I told you the butler wouldn't suit the work!"

"H-Have you solved the riddle y-yet?" the Rabbit pressed, putting its twitching nose almost in Holmes's face.

"No," the detective scowled, leaning back in his chair. "What's the answer?"

"I haven't the s-slightest idea," the Rabbit tittered, then looked past Holmes to the sudden commotion which had broken out further down the table. "H-How do you think those two are g-getting on?"

Holmes followed the Rabbit's gaze. Oh, for pity's sake, they were at it again! And the Unicorn clearly had the upper hand this time, the Lion gasping for breath, bleeding profusely from a dozen wounds, its once smart black suit hanging in tatters... and the crown lying all but forgotten beneath the Unicorn's trampling hooves...

Twinkle, twinkle, royal hat...

...the candlelight gleaming off its wickedly sharp horn as it lunged forward...

How I wonder where you're at...

~0~

Holmes woke with a start, heart drumming frantically in his chest. God in heaven... *what* a nightmare! The detective shuddered, passing a shaking hand over his face, then propped himself up on his elbow. He appeared to be back in his room at the manor, fully dressed under the counterpane besides his jacket and shoes. Had Watson put him to bed? How long had he slept? The last thing he remembered clearly was drinking tea in

Reverend Heyer's parlour... and after that, nothing, besides a vague impression of sunlight on leaves...

There was a quiet tap at the door. "Holmes?" Watson's voice came softly. "Are you awake?"

"Come in, Watson." Holmes sat up and reached for the glass of water that had been left on the bedside table, his throat was horribly dry.

"Feeling better, old chap?" Watson set a laden tray on the table. "You've been snoring your head off since it touched the pillow!"

Holmes flushed, torn between gratitude and embarrassment at his own weakness. "What time is it?"

"Four o'clock, you've been asleep three hours. The police got here before we did – don't worry, I brought you up the back stairs," Watson added hastily as Holmes's eyes widened in horror. "They've taken charge of Brunton's body, and Musgrave handed over those silver coins as well. Inspector Knightley's been taking statements from everyone in the house. He'll be wanting yours, of course, when you're feeling up to it. Jam tart?"

"And Rachel Howells?" Holmes persisted, ignoring the plate Watson held out and throwing off the bedclothes. "What's become of her?"

"Well, she's conscious..." Watson hesitated, expression troubled. "I haven't informed Knightley of it, though. Perhaps it was presumptuous of me, but... he seemed just a little too much like our colleagues at the Yard for my liking!"

"Watson?" Holmes looked up from tying his shoes. "What is it? What have you found out?"

"Nurse Woolsey... discovered something in Rachel's room this morning." Watson sighed heavily. "Holmes, she'd been knitting." As the detective's brow furrowed in bewilderment, "She's *pregnant*, Holmes, three months gone. I examined her myself with the nurse as witness."

"A child!" Holmes breathed, closing his eyes as several pieces of the puzzle fell into place. And that begged the question of who else had known – had Brunton? "We may need to question the local doctor next, see what he can tell us."

"Well... there *is* someone who might know more," Watson said. "Rachel appears to have been a devout Catholic, and with a kindly priest in the vicinity..."

Holmes nodded slowly. Yes, Reverend Heyer might indeed have heard Rachel's confession. He did seem the sort to whom a fragile young woman might turn for advice without driving her to despair, the caterpillar incident had certainly... dear God... *the caterpillar... the butterfly... "H-Have you solved the riddle y-yet?" ...the Unicorn's eyes blazing with rage, the dying snarls of the Lion...* "The Lion!" Of course, of *course*, it all fit!

"Lion? Where?" Musgrave appeared in the bedroom door, smiling. "Dreaming about that old rhyme, were you, Holmes?"

"Yes," Holmes replied with a faint smile of his own. "Not a very pleasant experience, but valuable all the same. Do take a seat, Musgrave. Watson, I should be much obliged if you would lock the door." Watson looked at Holmes strangely, but obeyed. "And now, my dear Musgrave," the detective continued pleasantly, "perhaps you would be good enough to tell us what *really* happened last night."

Musgrave blinked. "What? Good God, Holmes, must we go through all that again? I've already told you..."

"A pack of lies!" Holmes snapped. "Oh, I've no doubt you did catch Brunton examining your family document, but even *you* can't have been stupid enough not to draw the obvious conclusion: that your loyal butler had worked out the Musgrave secret, and had every intention of profiting from it himself with never a word to you, the rightful heir! He'd even asked you for the elm's height a few days earlier!" He noted Musgrave's paling features with grim satisfaction, and went on. "Why *did* you then dismiss Brunton, Musgrave? Was it to make him desperate, spur him into finding the treasure for you before he left, while you and the other servants watched his every move? You didn't expect him to go after it that very night in the rain, did you, with no sun or moon to point the way? No wonder you were so eager to find him when you heard he'd vanished!" Holmes stepped closer, voice low and menacing: "Or perhaps... you had already found him, and Rachel Howells bears no guilt but that of a bastard child..."

"Don't call it...!" Musgrave burst out, then froze, eyes like a cornered deer.

"As I thought," Holmes nodded, exchanging a significant look with Watson. "How long *has* Brunton been your rival, then? When Rachel first came to Hurlstone?" *White Queen to Red Knight...*

"A year ago," mumbled Musgrave. "Oh, Holmes, you should have seen her! Such fire in those deep, dark eyes, eyes a man might drown in..."

"When you've *quite* finished rhapsodising, Musgrave?" Holmes broke in acidly on the lordling's nauseating reverie. "But her affections already lay with your butler, so you did everything in your power to come between them, including spreading the vile rumour that he had strayed with your gamekeeper's daughter! And when she came to you, her employer, for counsel, you seduced her in the guise of comforter and friend."

"Seduced!" Musgrave laughed bitterly. "Much you know about it, Holmes! She fell into my bed like a ripe piece of fruit!"

"And will now be *bearing* fruit in March," Watson replied in an even tone, but his tightening jaw muscles a clear indicator to Holmes of how close the doctor was to letting fly with his fists. "Whose is it, yours or Brunton's?"

"She won't say," Musgrave muttered. "Damned us both to Hell and declared it was none of our business!"

"A very wise course of action, under the circumstances," Holmes remarked. Keeping Musgrave in suspense had ensured that Rachel would keep her place, and Brunton, too... Was that why Heyer had been such a regular visitor to the manor: Musgrave attempting to worm the secret out of him? "But with the unintended consequence that you two have been jostling for position in her esteem ever since, even in front of guests! You must have been delighted at catching Brunton red-handed, giving you a watertight excuse to dismiss him! What were you planning to do once he'd found the treasure? Did you have any intention of sharing the spoils, or the credit for the discovery? I can't imagine Brunton had any confidence that you would!"

"Which means, Holmes, that Musgrave can't have been with Brunton when he found it," Watson hastened to add. "It's just as you said: he trusted Rachel, not Musgrave. He'd never have gone down that hole with his former master standing over it!"

"Exactly!" Musgrave said eagerly, seeming not to care for the moment that he was exchanging the brand of murderer for that of a cad. "Whatever you may think, gentlemen, I certainly didn't want Brunton dead. Rachel would never have forgiven me! I-I was even going to write him a magnificent character before he left, he'd have easily found a new position!"

"Don't look for any sympathy here, Musgrave," growled Watson, coming forward with clenched fists. "You were only too eager to lay the blame for Brunton's death at Rachel's feet! Was it because you knew she wouldn't hang, being with child? Maybe you intended to speak for her at the trial, claim her sinful pregnancy to a philanderer had affected her wits. You could nobly adopt the child as your heir in the eyes of the world, leaving Rachel little choice but to marry you!"

"That will do, Watson," Holmes said quietly, laying a restraining hand on the doctor's arm. Musgrave's white face and trembling lips were proof enough for the pair of them, but it would hardly stand up in a court of law. "We have more pressing concerns just now. Inspector Knightley has only one suspect for a possible murder thus far, and Rachel's condition will not save her from prison. We must discover, once and for all, how that stone fell!" Holmes turned to the shaken lordling, voice stern. "You don't deserve *any* consideration, Musgrave. Your cowardice and lies have already cost two people their happiness, and one of them his life. But you may yet save your family's honour by saving the woman you claimed to love from a life in chains. Will you come?"

~0~

"Mr. Musgrave, Dr. Watson." Inspector Knightley rose from his chair as the trio entered the library. "And this must be Mr. Sherlock Holmes. It's an honour to meet you, sir."

"Likewise, Inspector," Holmes replied, noting in wry amusement that Knightley's wary expression was a great deal more eloquent than his tongue. "It was my pleasure to assist in clearing up this little matter."

Knightley snorted at the description, then shook his head, looking faintly sheepish. "Well, I will say you three have already done a great deal of the legwork for this *investigation*, Mr. Holmes, and I'm grateful. Is there any sign yet of the original chart that the butler copied?"

"No. Wherever it came from, Brunton most likely destroyed it, to guard against anyone else making the same connections he did." (Holmes felt rather than saw Musgrave's blush.) "Speaking of connections, Inspector, I am happy to report that Mr. Musgrave has just received fresh intelligence on the relationship between Richard Brunton and Rachel Howells. It appears that the rumours of Brunton's recent infidelity with Janet Tregellis were a mere fabrication, spread by some malicious person in the hope of ending the pair's engagement – which they sadly succeeded in doing."

Knightley raised a very Holmesian eyebrow, taking out a notebook and pencil. "Thank you, Mr. Musgrave, that ties in with the statement I received from Miss Tregellis this afternoon. She seemed as upset as any of the other staff to hear of Brunton's death, but not grief-stricken as one might expect, and she vehemently denied that he'd ever paid court to her of any kind. I don't suppose you would be willing to name the gossipmonger?"

"I'd be only too glad, Inspector," Musgrave said, blush deepening, "but my informant refused to give the culprit's name. I can't really fault them for not wishing to cost someone their employment, especially when others assisted in perpetuating the rumour – myself included, I regret to say."

"And, sadly, there are simply too many staff at Hurlstone to determine which of them may have been jealous enough of Brunton's position," Holmes interjected smoothly. "It hardly seems likely that they will commit such an act again, however, or that they were involved in last night's treasure hunt."

"Ah, yes." As Holmes had hoped, the mention of treasure at once turned Knightley's line of thought from innuendo to facts. "Which reminds me, Dr. Watson: is Rachel Howells ready for questioning yet, in your professional opinion?"

Holmes's eyes narrowed as Watson visibly bristled at Knightley's tone of impatient disdain. "I believe she is," the doctor answered with commendable restraint, "but I must still emphasise the need for delicacy, Inspector. Her condition..."

"Many thanks for the advice, Doctor," Knightley interrupted, drawing himself up. "You're a credit to your profession, but Miss Howells is still *my* prisoner, you know!"

"And *my* patient!" Watson retorted sharply. "As is her unborn child! So if you're planning on taking her away in handcuffs, Knightley, you'd best make that a cell for three! Sentence first, verdict after – is that the way of things in these parts?"

"Your chivalry is commendable, Watson," Holmes hastened to interject as Knightley drew a deep breath, "but a trifle premature, perhaps. Musgrave, will you kindly ring the bell? I think we could all use some refreshment. Join us, Inspector?"

~0~

Mercifully, tea and a plate of ham sandwiches did go a long way towards dispelling the gathering storm clouds in the room. "Consider this, Inspector," ventured Holmes, once the company had eaten and drunk their fill. "Brunton could hardly have enlisted Rachel's aid without persuading her that he had been falsely accused, and that whatever treasure they found would serve to build a new life together, away from Hurlstone." Was it worth telling Knightley about the chess set? Holmes could see from here that no other pieces had been disturbed since Rachel's Queen... but perhaps not. They had no solid evidence there, either, and Knightley clearly wasn't interested in any theories that sounded more fanciful than his own just now.

"Why, then, would she suddenly take it into her head once more that he was playing her false, and leave him for dead – the father of her child, no less?" Well, one of two candidates, anyhow...

"And don't forget that we never found the treasure in Rachel's possession," Musgrave added truthfully, if not entirely honestly – they never had looked for it beyond the cellar, after all! "How could she have had the presence of mind, after committing such a *crime passionel*, to hide the contents of a large chest well enough to deceive a keen observer like Sherlock Holmes? We all saw how distressed she was when it looked as though Brunton had abandoned her!"

"Well, as you say, Mr. Musgrave, appearances can be deceiving," Knightley smiled knowingly. "Miss Howells is Welsh, after all, with a passionate, Celtic soul. If the brain fever was caused by her anguished belief that Brunton had wronged her – an illness you tell me she's still recovering from, Doctor! – who can say what smouldering fire of vengeance suddenly sprang into flame when she saw him in her power? As to this supposed treasure, what proof have we got that Brunton found anything at all besides those two silver coins, which he hadn't even bothered to pocket, or to clean? Not to impugn your family's honour, Mr. Musgrave, but it's equally possible that anything of real value in that chest was long gone by the time your butler got there! Such crushing disappointment could easily lead to harsh words between the pair, or rash deeds..."

"Well, I shan't deny that your theory holds together, Inspector," Holmes said slowly, a sick feeling growing in the pit of his stomach to match the dismayed expressions of his colleagues. Much as it pained him to admit it... Knightley could very well have just solved the case! *Why* hadn't he so much as considered that some other thief might have deciphered the Ritual first and plundered the vault?! And heaven only knew how long ago that could have been: decades, or even centuries! What if Sir Ralph Musgrave had passed down the secret to an heir who valued wealth over fealty, and had merely preserved the Ritual for the sake of appearances? "As yet, however, all of our theories and evidence are mostly abstract. Let us hope that Miss Howells can throw some more light upon the matter."

"Now, there, Mr. Holmes, we're in total agreement," Knightley said eagerly, rising from his chair. "Oh, don't worry, Doctor: Mr. Holmes will be present as witness, I'm sure he'll attest to my humane treatment of your patient."

"Very well," Watson nodded grudgingly. "And in the meantime, Mr. Musgrave and I shall consult with Miss Howells's usual physician, inquire into the possibility of her spending the rest of her pregnancy at a sanatorium. *If* you're not satisfied as to her innocence after questioning, Inspector, a few month's delay before the trial will do no harm. I imagine the court would be lenient in its verdict, anyhow, but we still must get Rachel away from Hurlstone. If you'll pardon my saying so, Musgrave, this house practically reeks of centuries-old secrets and intrigues, it can't be healthy for her or the baby."

"N-no, not at all, quite right!" Musgrave stammered. "I ought to have considered that myself. Don't forget to tell Rachel about that when you see her, Inspector."

"I'll be sure to mention it," Knightley answered dryly, pocketing his notebook, and inclining his head to Musgrave with an odd little smile. "It's most generous of your lordship, I will say, under the circumstances. After you, gentlemen."

~0~

The footmen guarding Rachel's door had long since been relieved by one of Knightley's constables, who stiffened back to attention as the four men came into view, staring blankly at the opposite wall. Watson hid a smile as he caught a whiff of cigarette smoke – he ought to know himself how deadly dull sentry duty could be!

"Mr. Holmes and I will see Miss Howells now, Pike." Knightley gestured impatiently for the man to unlock the door. "Nurse Woolsey can accompany Mr. Musgrave and Dr. Watson."

"Begging your pardon, sir, but which nurse d'you mean?" said Constable Pike apologetically, fishing a small golden key out of his pocket. "The day nurse has already gone, her replacement came half an hour ago."

"Replacement?" Watson frowned. "I didn't know the night nurse was already here! She should have..." Oh *no*...

"Get that door open, Pike, on the double!" Knightley snapped, as the wide-eyed constable jammed the key into the lock. "Hurry it up, man!" But the Inspector must have known as well as the rest of them what they would find: Nurse Woolsey lying under the blankets on Rachel's narrow bed, eyes closed, her breathing the slow, heavy breath of the sedated, and no sign of her erstwhile charge or the new arrival.

Watson saw his medical bag standing open on the bureau and checked the contents. "Looks like the sleeping pills have been opened – this bottle isn't as tightly corked." He took out his stethoscope and listened to Woolsey's heartbeat: slow but steady, she'd likely wake next morning with no ill effects. But poor Rachel... If only he *had* let Holmes question her sooner! Would she still have been desperate enough to flee if she'd known the detective was acting on her behalf?

"And that jug of water on the table is almost empty," Holmes noted, doing an admirable job of suppressing his frustration for the moment – Knightley was certainly swearing enough under his breath for everyone just now.

"I'm sure I'm very sorry, sirs," Pike stammered, "but the Inspector never gave me no orders not to let the *nurses* through!"

Holmes nodded ruefully. "Don't be too hard on yourself, Constable. I suppose you never actually saw Rachel Howells's face when you were stationed outside the room, or Nurse Woolsey's? Then you couldn't have known it was Miss Howells leaving the room, especially if she had on the new arrival's apron and cap!" The detective crossed to the window and examined the catch. "And since they couldn't *both* walk out of the room without arousing suspicion..." He opened the window and peered down. "She must have waited until the other woman reached the ground, then shut the window after her. It's not as difficult a climb as one might suppose, although there is a deep impression in the soil of the flower bed below – she was fortunate it rained last night, with that far to fall!"

"But who was she, then, this woman?" Musgrave said dazedly, finding his voice at last. "And why would she risk helping Rachel escape?"

"Never mind *that* now!" Knightley thundered, red-faced. "Thanks to the good doctor's mollycoddling, we now have *two* fugitives to apprehend! You can go and round up the other men, Pike, since you've proven yourself such a marvellous escort! Mr. Musgrave, what dogs do you have around the place?"

~0~

"I did tell you, Inspector," Musgrave sighed. The four stood with Keeper Tregellis amid a milling pack of dogs on the back lawn, who were mostly sniffing excitedly around the men's knees rather than the ground. "They're all *gun* dogs, not bloodhounds! Unless Rachel and her companion have suddenly grown feathers, they probably won't be much help."

"Oh no?" smiled Knightley. The nearest dogs to the woods had stiffened at a sudden shout. "We'll just see, shall we?"

"Inspector!" Pike and another constable came running out of the trees. "The pool, sir! We've found something!"

"The women's tracks?" Knightley said eagerly, shooting a smug glance at his colleagues.

140

"...Hard to say, sir. You'd better come see for yourself."

As they reached the pool, Watson's heart sank like the proverbial stone. A steep bank overlooked the deepest water, where a single trail of footprints ended abruptly, the soil at the very edge ploughed up into a patch of mud, the plants torn and bedraggled... "Merciful God... Oh, Holmes, you don't think... Holmes?" But Watson was talking to the empty air at his elbow, the detective nowhere in sight.

"Inspector, did you see..." The doctor trailed off; Knightley was far too busy issuing orders for dragging the pool to have noticed a thing. "*Holmes!*" Wonderful! Where had the damn fool run off to now?

~0~

Holmes braced his palms against the stones of the cellar stairwell, keeping as far to the left as he could. With no light to carry, he needed the best possible footing on these steps; it wouldn't do to slip and make a sound now! Not that he was overly worried about that, as whoever had reached the cellar before him (carelessly leaving the connecting door unlocked) was making a considerable racket themselves: a chorus of wooden thumps and clatters, punctuated by grunts of effort.

Another turn, and the flickering light of a lantern appeared on the walls; one more, and Holmes was peering cautiously around the central pillar into the room. A slender, muffled figure was rifling through the remaining piles of wood on hands and knees, dragging logs and billets away from the walls and throwing them towards the centre of the room, quite a few going down the hole in the floor.

"Good evening, Miss Tregellis." The stranger stiffened and whipped around, eyes and pupils wide in the lamplight, a few strands of fair, curly hair escaping from under her hat. "I do hope I'm not disturbing you," Holmes continued pleasantly, stepping further into the room. "Please, continue. I blush to confess it took me far too long to realise the treasure had never left the cellar at all – thanks in part to Inspector Knightley's notion of an earlier thief. How much *did* Miss Howells promise you in return for her freedom?"

"*Not a penny!*" a second female voice shrieked behind the detective, and a solid shove to the small of Holmes's back sent him sprawling on the flagstones, his head just over the hole.

"That's enough, Rachel!" Janet's voice came sharply. "Stop! And now, sir, if you'll kindly climb down into that hole?" Holmes looked up with a groan of pain to see the woman levelling a pistol at him. "I don't want to shoot you, but we really can't afford to take chances just now. And don't think for a moment that I wouldn't, Mr. Holmes," as he hesitated. "Having a gamekeeper for a father has its uses, and no one will hear the shot from upstairs."

Holmes took in the woman's expression – sad but calm, and utterly resolved – and nodded slowly, trying hard to ignore the flutter of panic in his gut at the thought of being trapped down here in the dark, just like Brunton... He would be found soon enough with Watson heading the search, surely! "If you give me your word not to replace the stone completely, madam, I shall comply."

The detective could have boxed his own ears for those careless words as Janet's eyes flashed in anger, and a hiccoughing sob came from behind him. "My God... do you really think I'd ask *that* of Rachel, after what happened?" The woman waited until Holmes had gingerly lowered himself and found his footing amongst the fallen wood, then took a small bottle from her pocket and dropped it down to him. "Drink it. We'll have time to escape before you raise the alarm, and no one needs to move that stone again."

"Would it be indelicate, then, to ask either of you what did happen here?" Holmes made himself as comfortable as he could on the billets, grateful for a seat that wasn't freezing stone. He uncorked the bottle – the last of the stolen sleeping pills, no doubt – raised it in salute to his captors, and downed the contents.

"That's not my secret to tell, Mr. Holmes." Janet left Holmes's line of sight for a few moments, returning slowly, hand in hand with a pale and trembling Rachel Howells. "You've no idea how brave she's been, just coming back to this room!" Janet smiled warmly at Rachel, putting her arm around the maid's waist in a sisterly embrace. "I probably could have got you down that hole alone – you fell for the searching act, after all – but she chose not to risk it. And your doctor friend thinks he's doing her a *favour*, shutting her away like china in a cabinet? You men aren't fit to wipe her boots, any of you!"

"I'm inclined to agree," Holmes answered softly, his head and limbs already becoming leaden. "You... have the treasure, then? May I see it?" He would have to content himself this time... with knowing that at least... his deductions... had been correct...

"You can do more than that, Mr. Hoolmess..." Janet gave him an enigmatic smile from what suddenly seemed a very long way away, and produced a stained linen bag from inside her cloak. "Youuu caaan keeep iiiiit..."

~0~

"Holmes?" Watson had chosen not to watch the dragging at the lake, hugging himself against the growing chill of the autumn air as he emerged from the trees. Neither he nor Holmes had thought to don overcoats before going out to the kennels, and it was nearly dark. He hadn't noticed Holmes slip away, so the most logical conclusion was that the detective had simply headed back the way they'd come. The doctor hoped someone at the house had actually seen him, the place was a rabbit warren! "Holmes!"

"*Aw! Aw!*" came a croaking echo somewhere to his right, then the owner of the voice flew out of the shadows and landed on the grass.

Watson had to smile. "Hullo, Jack! I don't suppose *you've* seen my friend, have you?"

"*Aw!*" Jack Tar shook his wings and took off again in the direction of the old manor wing, landing a few yards further away and cocking his head expectantly at Watson, almost as if...

"I must be dreaming," Watson murmured in bewilderment. Still, no harm in seeing what came of it if he was! And if he wasn't... "All right, old fellow, lead on!"

~0~

"So, you didn't make *any* attempt whatever to stop them?!" Knightley's face was turning a fetching shade of magenta.

"*Kindly* roar at a more civilised volume, Inspector?" grimaced Holmes, slowly sitting up in bed. Those sleeping pills had left him with a splitting headache and a mouthful of cotton on waking the next morning. "Well, they did have me at rather a disadvantage." He'd like to have seen Knightley fare any better!

"And that, Holmes, is the sanest thing I've heard you say all week," Watson said sternly, handing the detective a glass of water. "I declare, you've no more sense than a baby sometimes! Running off without a word to anyone, with a possible killer on the loose – what on earth were you thinking?"

"Watson, whatever else Rachel Howells may be," Holmes said gravely, ignoring the doctor's question, "she is *not* a murderess, cold-blooded or otherwise. What I saw of that blessed woman in the cellar last night contradicts every one of your theories, Inspector. She was genuinely insulted at my suggestion that she had bribed Miss Tregellis to help her escape, so it hardly seems likely that she and Brunton could have fallen out again over money! As for the idea that the aftermath of Rachel's illness caused her to momentarily forget that they had reconciled... how do you reconcile that theory with a woman of sound enough heart and mind to return to the room where her fiancé had died less than a day earlier, in order to protect Miss Tregellis?"

"By striking you down from behind, don't forget!" Knightley exclaimed.

"There is a world of difference between pushing someone in the back and clubbing them over the head, Inspector. Before last night, Rachel only ever knew me as her employer's friend and guest; how was she to know that I was not as convinced of her guilt as you? Given the circumstances, her restraint was commendable."

Holmes smiled sadly as Watson reddened and looked away. "And there is no guarantee that Rachel would have remained if I had spoken to her any sooner, Watson. What reassurance could I have given her? We found no conclusive evidence in the cellar to prove that she did not deliberately strike the support away from the flagstone. In any case, a jury would probably take one look at the contents of that linen bag and draw the simplest conclusion."

"Erm..." Watson gave his friend an odd look. "Holmes, have you... actually looked in the bag yet?"

"No, I hadn't time before..." Oh no... "Watson? What *did* you find?"

"We're not sure," Watson answered carefully. "Musgrave's watching over it in the library, you can go down once you've – Holmes, you come back *this minute* and dress properly!"

~0~

Watson and Musgrave watched in sympathy as Holmes stared with furrowed brow at the contents of the bag, laid out on a tray: bent and broken pieces of rusted, blackened metal. The doctor could understand completely why Janet and Rachel had given them back! Knightley, meanwhile, was conferring out in the passage with Constable Pike, and from the set of the pair's shoulders, it wasn't good news there, either. (Although, if Watson were absolutely honest with himself, he wasn't all *that* upset over the case's outcome.)

"Unbelievable," Knightley groaned, stalking back in and casting himself down on the sofa. "Two fugitives slipped through our fingers – two *women*, at that! – and the Musgrave treasure turns out to be a worthless pile of scrap! We'll be the laughingstock of the county when this gets out!"

"Must it, Inspector?" Watson shrugged, eyebrows raised. "Janet and Rachel may be fugitives, but they're hardly dangerous criminals. When all's said and done, they haven't *really* harmed anyone, or stolen anything of value!"

"Well, Janet did drug Nurse Woolsey, and take Holmes hostage," ventured Musgrave.

"For Rachel's sake, Musgrave. I doubt you'll convince either of them to press charges. Brunton died by accident, as far as we can tell, and the treasure, such as it is, lies there." Watson rose and put a kindly hand on the rigid detective's shoulder. "I'm so sorry, Holmes. I know how disappointed you must be –"

"Is this *all* there was in the bag?" Holmes asked, abruptly coming back to life.

"Apart from a couple of pebbles at the bottom... Holmes?" The detective had sprung out of his chair and snatched up the discarded bag from the table, plunging his hand to the bottom and scrabbling in the corners. "Holmes, what on earth...?"

"A*ha!*" Holmes dropped the retrieved pebbles into the tray. "Watson, your handkerchief, if you please. Now, gentlemen, observe..." A few rubs at the largest of the dull-coloured stones, and it glowed like an ember in the light from the windows.

"A ruby!" Musgrave gasped.

"Good God..." Watson murmured; and a moment later, a pea-sized emerald was flashing green fire beside its cousin. "Holmes, *how* did you know?!"

"Because they couldn't have been anything else," Holmes answered, not even bothering to conceal his satisfaction, and waved an unabashedly dramatic hand over the tray. "I must congratulate you, Musgrave, on coming into possession of one of the greatest historical relics in our nation's history, albeit in such a tragic fashion."

"Well, what is it, then?" demanded Knightley.

"Nothing less than the ancient crown of the kings of England!"

"The crown!" Watson and Knightley exclaimed in thunderstruck unison.

"...the *crown*..." Poor Musgrave looked as if he might faint.

"Precisely. Consider the Ritual – how did it run? 'Whose was it?' 'His who is gone.' "

"The execution of Charles the First!" Watson said excitedly.

Holmes nodded, continuing: " 'Who shall have it?' 'He who will come.' Charles the Second, whose advent was already foreseen. There can, I think, be no doubt that this battered and broken diadem once encircled the brows of the royal Stuarts. When the royal party fled after the death of the King, they probably left many of their most precious possessions behind them, with the intention of returning for them in more peaceful times."

"Stuff and nonsense!" Knightley scoffed. "If that's Charles the First's crown, then where's the gold? Look, the metal's all black and rusty, gold doesn't do that!"

Holmes snorted. "You thought the crown would be *solid* gold, Inspector? Imagine how heavy that would be to wear on state occasions! No, no, the crown was clearly gold leaf over steel. For best results, it ought to have been silver, but I suppose there simply wasn't enough to hand when it was made. And now we see the end result of such shoddy workmanship: the gold plating is completely gone, eaten by the fungi in that chest for over two centuries..."

"Which could also explain why there weren't any pearls left," Musgrave sighed. "But *why* didn't my family simply return the crown to Charles the Second? More to the point, why is it in pieces? Rust alone didn't do this!"

"Ah, now that we may never answer. It might well have come into Sir Ralph's possession in that state, broken up by thieves, perhaps, or enemies of the King... And your ancestor most likely died without ever explaining the Ritual's meaning to his descendants – a simple, thoughtless oversight... until at last it came within reach of a man who tore its secret out of it, and lost his life in the venture."

"Poor devil!" Watson murmured. Had Brunton had any idea of what a priceless artefact he'd held, for all of a minute? And what effect would the news have on Rachel, finally learning what had really been in that bag... But then... good God, why were none of them considering what *else* might have been in there last night?! There could easily have been more than two jewels, or more coins than the ones Holmes had found in the chest... Then Watson noticed Holmes looking up at him intently, giving a little shake of his head. No... no, quite right. What they had found in the bag and chest was all there had ever been, of course it was.

The doctor pressed his lips together for a moment, meeting Holmes's gaze steadily, then turned towards the sideboard. "Brandy, gentlemen? I rather think we've earned it." Handing snifters out to the other three took Watson past the fireplace, and a casual glance at the chess board on the mantel stopped him dead, eyes wide: *both* Queens were now missing! Not only that, but the remaining Red Knight appeared to be in a standoff with its white counterparts, the White King skulking in the corner behind the pair, guarded by the rook...

"Mail's arrived, Holmes!" Watson called, walking into the sitting room. "Looks like the usual."

"Thank you, Watson," Holmes answered absently, attention fixed on the rack of test tubes in front of him. "On the table, please."

Watson obliged, then sat down at the writing desk and returned to his notebook. Eight months had passed since their return from Sussex, arriving home just in time to make enough of a dent in Holmes's case files to appease Mrs. Hudson when *she* came back, noticeably mellower after a week spent at the seaside. Holmes had also kept his promise to Watson in allowing him to write up some of the detective's earliest cases; *The Adventure of the Gloria Scott* had been published in last month's issue of the Strand, and was still selling well.

A letter had arrived from Hurlstone that December, Reginald Musgrave contritely thanking the pair once more for their assistance and discretion. Her Majesty the Queen had graciously permitted the pieces of crown and remaining coins to be displayed at the manor, a plaque inside the case giving Richard Brunton full credit for the discovery. *It means little enough in the face of Brunton's tragic end, perhaps,* Musgrave wrote, *but at least his memory can be honoured...* Holmes privately suspected that Musgrave's chief concern was the increased revenue which the sudden influx of sightseers had brought to the region. Meanwhile, the elder Tweed brother had stepped up to fill the butler's position, and was coming along promisingly.

The hunt for Rachel and Janet (of whom nothing more had been heard) was now at an end, Musgrave wrote further. Inspector Knightley had eventually heeded Watson's counsel; the two women, wherever they were, would certainly take care to live as model citizens henceforth, and there was also Rachel's unborn child to think of. Holmes had caught a hint of wistfulness in Musgrave's words there, but couldn't find it in him to be sympathetic. If the lordling truly wished for a wife, or an heir, he could court the next woman through honest means.

On a similar but happier note, Reverend Heyer had recently published his treatise on local customs, and was now courting Miss Hatfield! Watson had chuckled in delight at that, ignoring Holmes's sigh of resignation, although the detective couldn't help wondering if the more practical-minded charwoman had set events in motion herself...

Musgrave had even given his reluctant blessing, after a great deal of reflection, for their shared adventure to be published. Watson had read between the lines with a grin, and written back to reassure Musgrave that there was no rush, he'd jot down what he could remember when he had a moment... but now, in May, Watson wasn't any nearer to deciding which details were safe to include in the story, or even what title to use.

" 'The Musgrave Ritual' might work?" Holmes suggested, Watson's tutting and muttering behind him finally breaking through his concentration.

"You *must* be bored!" Watson laughed. "No, that's just what the title of the case is *called*. The title really *is* 'The Adventure of the Twinkling Hat.' "

Holmes looked up at the doctor strangely. "So... that's the name of the adventure, then?"

"No, that's quite another thing! The *adventure* is called 'The Lion and the Unicorn'; but that's only what it's *called*, you know!"

"Well, what *is* the adventure, then?" said Holmes, by this time completely bewildered.

"I was coming to that," Watson huffed. "The adventure really *is* 'Malice Underground' – and I'll thank you not to ask any more childish questions."

"...Madness is catching, I see," was all Holmes could think of in response, giving up on his experiments for the moment to open his mail. Ah, now this one looked especially interesting...

~0~

Mr. Holmes,

I'm sure you remember the woman who pointed a gun at your head in the cellar at Hurlstone. Whatever regrets I may have over a necessary course of action, I'm not writing to ask for forgiveness for my part in the affair. If it was up to me, I wouldn't

waste a drop of ink writing to you, not when my own father is in
far greater need of reassuring news. But Rachel insisted that you
and Dr. Watson deserved to know the truth, after everything you
two <u>tried</u> to do to help her, and since she won't be strong enough
to use a pen for a few more weeks, she asked me to write it for
her. God help me, I never could refuse her anything. But then
neither could Richard Brunton.

Rachel is sitting up in bed while I write this, watching her
son wave his tiny fists in the cradle. You can tell Dr. Watson that
the new doctor still won't let her nurse him, but he thinks the wet
nurse won't be needed many more weeks if Rachel keeps going
on like she is now. The baby is well, too, stronger and heartier
than either of us dared hope for. We've called him... well, I'm
sure you can guess his name. Rachel has just sharply reminded
me that that pig Musgrave doesn't need to know for certain who
the father is, not from anyone. I can't tell you how good it is to
see her getting back enough strength to scold <u>someone</u>, even if it
isn't me she desperately wants to be arguing with.

I didn't know the late Mrs. Brunton very well, but I do know
she'd been ill for a long time. Consumption, everyone whispered
– the same damn whispers that nearly did for Rachel. Richard

was heartbroken when she died, and yes, he did look for comfort with a few other women at first, but I was never one of them. From something he said once, I think he used to have a sister who looked a bit like me.

You never saw Rachel and Richard together in the same room, did you, Mr. Holmes? If you had, that might have made it all so much clearer. When Rachel came to work at Hurlstone, it was obvious from the beginning that no two people were better made for each other. Even when Rachel thought the worst about Richard and me (I still have a scar on my neck from the kettle she threw at my head), I was sure it was only a matter of time before she would relent and believe the truth from Richard's lips. He could have charmed the crows out of the trees with that tongue of his. If I had even suspected who really started that <u>wicked</u> lie... Well, maybe that was for the best. But Richard... Servants may be invisible to their so-called betters, Mr. Holmes, but not blind, especially to where their eyes and hands are going.

You already know most of what happened that awful night, and the next day, but I suppose it's best to tell you everything as we two know it. Richard woke Rachel in the middle of the night and swore on his knees that he'd never betrayed her, that

Musgrave had lied to get her into his bed, but it didn't matter anymore, he didn't care whose child it was. He'd been caught with the ritual paper by Musgrave and given a week's notice, so there was only that night to act. Whatever treasure was hiding under the stone would be Rachel's, she could do whatever she wanted with it: leave with him or on her own, or even stay at Hurlstone with Musgrave, if that would make her happy. Rachel threw herself into Richard's arms, finally believing him, and begged him to forgive her.

They lifted the stone by wedging firewood into the gap and propping it open. Yes, Mr. Holmes, Richard should have tipped it away from the hole. Hindsight is such a wonderfully useless thing, isn't it? I'm sure you've realised that there was more in that box than what was in the bag we left you. Richard was good at history, and he recognised the crown, even broken and covered in rust. But with all the gold gone, who could they sell it to, besides a museum? In the end, Richard thought it was wiser to leave the crown and some of the remaining jewels behind, to keep Musgrave from thinking he'd been cheated. He put everything he could find into the bag, meaning to sort through it all afterwards, and handed the bag up to Rachel. But it was too heavy, pulling her off balance. She reached out to save herself, and the closest thing to hand was the wood holding up the stone. It came loose under her weight, and the stone crashed down, just missing her foot.

Rachel tried, Mr. Holmes, she tried so hard to lift the stone with the scarf, but even with Richard pushing from underneath, it hardly moved. Richard must have shouted at her to run for help, I'm sure he must, but how could she have understood him through that thick stone in such a panic? She shouldn't have been exerting herself like that at all, pregnant and recovering from the brain fever. She must have fainted, because the next thing she knew, she was lying on top of the stone, and Richard had stopped shouting.

Can you imagine what that must have been like, Mr. Holmes? Knowing the one you loved most in the world was dead because you weren't strong enough to save them? Rachel doesn't remember much of what happened afterwards, except for shoving the bag behind some logs, and waking the next morning in her own bed. The whole thing must have seemed so crazy, I think she almost managed to convince herself she'd dreamed it, until Richard didn't come to breakfast with everyone else.

When Dad told me Richard had gone missing, I knew he wouldn't have just <u>left</u> Rachel, not without her telling him to. And why would she have told him that, if she was so upset about him being gone? Then Inspector Knightley came to tell us that he'd been found dead, and that you and Musgrave thought <u>Rachel</u> had murdered him! I tried to find you, Mr. Holmes, but you'd already gone to the Reverend's house, and Mr. Tweed wouldn't let me in to see Rachel. Somehow I didn't think it was worthwhile talking to Musgrave about Rachel before you came back, not when he seemed to believe along with everyone else that I'd stolen Richard from her.

It's too easy to forget, isn't it, how thin the upstairs walls of an old house can be? I'm not ashamed to admit I was listening in the next room when you and Dr. Watson made that pasty-faced little worm admit what he'd done and beg for mercy. That's a memory I'll treasure for years to come. Maybe one day I can even share it with Rachel. I am sorry for frightening everyone with those footprints at the pool, though. I couldn't be sure the police would find them, but it was worth a try, and dragging the bottom would have proved nobody was drowned soon enough. Of course, you didn't fall for it at all, did you? I saw you coming back later through the old hall window, looking right in our direction. I sent

Rachel to hide in the storerooms at the other end and waited for you below. After everything Rachel had been through, I didn't think for a moment she could face that cellar again! I'm proud to say she proved me as wrong about her as anyone. So did Mary Woolsey, if you can believe it.

When I threw a stone at the bedroom window, the nurse told me she already knew Rachel was innocent, but showing Dr. Watson the knitting she'd found hadn't helped anything, it just gave the police another reason to think Rachel might have done it, and Dr. Watson the idea of sending her to Holloway. I told Mary that I could get Rachel safely away with her help, and to drop her apron and cap down to me. That got me past the constable, then Mary took the sleeping pill willingly when I was inside, changing places with Rachel in the bed. When she was asleep, I climbed out the window and dropped down into the garden. Rachel closed the window, put on the apron and cap next, told the constable to open the door, and walked out right under his nose.

I don't think there's anything else you don't already know. Tell Dr. Watson he has Rachel's permission to tell her and Richard's story, though we both know there'll be a lot he has to leave out. Sometimes I wish you'd made Musgrave confess to Inspector Knightley, too, or that I was brave enough to write one more letter... But whenever I'm tempted, I remember the whole truth could hurt many more people than just him. I hate to think how much trouble Dad is in already, with me being wanted by the police. I won't have him losing his job because of me, or any of my friends at Hurlstone. At least now there's enough people who know what happened that the future Mrs. Musgrave, whoever she is, has nothing to fear from her husband.

Yours sincerely,
Janet Tregellis

~0~

Watson took the pages Holmes solemnly handed to him, read them twice through, then blew his nose hard. "My God..." he said at last, huskily. That *poor* girl! '*...the one you loved most in the world was dead because you weren't strong enough to save them...*' And then Rachel had gone *back* to that very spot, to help the woman who had actually rescued her... *"You men aren't fit to wipe her boots, any of you!"* As much as Watson hated to admit

166

it, Miss Tregellis was right: what *had* he and Holmes really done to help anyone that day, besides the person who least deserved it?

"We cleared a good man's name, Watson," Holmes said softly, correctly divining his friend's thoughts from his dismal expression. "And whatever else we failed to do, Janet Tregellis's letter will soon set to rights in Inspector Knightley's hands – with a few redactions, of course."

"Of course," sighed Watson, setting the letter down. "Still... And it certainly hasn't made writing up the case any easier! How on earth am I going to explain Musgrave's role in any of it without making him seem like a bounder or a fool?"

"When given a choice of evils, choose the lesser," Holmes quipped innocently. "Musgrave protested hard enough that the Ritual was nonsense, let that be what he truly believes in the story."

"I suppose..." Although that would probably mean leaving Reverend Heyer out of the story, too. Perhaps Musgrave ought to come to Baker Street himself, rather than write. Speaking of things left out, though... Why hadn't Janet mentioned moving those other chess pieces before escaping the manor with Rachel? Had she merely forgotten such a trifling detail in the intervening time, or...

Brinnnggg!

"A gentleman to see you, Mr. Holmes," Mrs. Hudson announced a minute later, presenting the caller's card.

" 'Mr. Cyril Overton,' " read Holmes, handing it to Watson next. "Handwritten with a most inferior fountain pen, save for the crest, which I believe to be that of Cambridge University. By all means, Mrs. Hudson, send him up."

The card was soon followed by its sender. Watson's brows shot up as an enormous young man, sixteen stone of solid bone and muscle, spanned the doorway with his broad shoulders, comely features haggard with anxiety. "Mr. Sherlock Holmes? Inspector Hopkins at the Yard told me to come. He thought this was more in your line than the regular police."

"Pray sit down, Mr. Overton," Holmes replied soothingly, "and tell us what the matter is. My friend and colleague, Dr.

Watson," he added as the young giant seated himself. "My work has never yet taken me into the field of amateur athletics, but even I was aware while at Oxford of the fierce rivalry between our respective schools in sporting matters."

"You're dead right there, Mr. Holmes," Overton exclaimed in astonishment. "Well, I've nothing to say against Oxford's team, but that's just the trouble! Godfrey Staunton – you've heard of him, of course? He's simply the hinge that our whole team turns on. Whether it's drives, split shots or canons, there's no one to touch him; and then, he's got the head and can hold us all together. Without him in tomorrow's match, we're sunk!"

"Wait a minute," Watson frowned. "Canons? *Split* shots? There's nothing like that in rugby... is there?" There hadn't been when *he'd* last played!

Cyril Overton's forehead wrinkled. "Rugby? Who said anything... D'you mean to tell me, Dr. Watson, that you don't know Godfrey Staunton, the crack striker of Blackheath? Good Lord, where have you lived?"

"I fear, Mr. Overton," ventured Holmes, lips twitching, "that Dr. Watson and I are not quite so well-acquainted with the noble sport of croquet as one might assume. However, your visit proves that even in that world of fresh air and fair play there may be work for us to do, so please continue..."

The End

Also from Claire Daines

What if two had perished at Reichenbach Falls? One simple, disastrous error throws Sherlock Holmes from his intended Hiatus into a tortuous journey of sorrow and remorse. Far from home, broken in body and spirit, the haunted detective fights to survive the single most tragic failure of his career - a fight he cannot win alone. With old and new companions beside him, and a threat as deadly as Moriarty in pursuit, Holmes must find a way to live on without his greatest friend, while saving the rest of his beloved adopted family from a similar fate.

Christmas Eve, 1890. Thanks to the tireless pursuit of Sherlock Holmes, Professor Moriarty's criminal empire stands on a knife edge. Still, three ghostly visitors may yet convince the Napoleon of Crime that his destiny lies in another direction...